WESTERN

BAD!

SA

3558

WITHDRAWN

STACKS

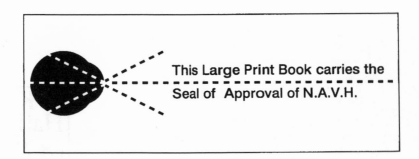

This Large Print Book carries the
Seal of Approval of N.A.V.H.

SAVAGE SIERRA

T.V. Olsen

G.K. Hall & Co.
Thorndike, Maine

Published in 1998 by arrangement with
Golden West Literary Agency.

G.K. Hall Large Print Paperback Series.

The text of this Large Print edition is unabridged.
Other aspects of the book may vary from the original edition.

Set in 16 pt. Plantin by Rick Gundberg.

Printed in the United States on permanent paper.

Library of Congress Cataloging in Publication Data

Olsen, Theodore V.
    Savage Sierra / T.V. Olsen.
        p. (large print) cm.
    ISBN 0-7838-8420-6 (lg. print : sc : alk. paper)
    1. Large type books. I. Title.
[PS3565.L8S28   1998]
    813′.54—dc21   97-50194

SAVAGE SIERRA

CHAPTER ONE

Frowning over an account book spread open on a rear counter, the sutler glanced up without much interest as Angsman entered the post store. Recognizing the newcomer then, Harley Moffat's bright swift eyes glinted with surprise and pleasure, not quite canceled by his dry greeting:

"Hello, you damned recluse."

"Harley."

Angsman paused in the cool mingled odors of leather and bolt cloth and foodstuffs, then came across the room, his moccasined tread noiseless and catlike. Angsman's towering and big-boned frame was dried to lean rawhide by desert heat and wind. He wore ragged duck trousers and a calico shirt long-faded to an indeterminate neutral color, a battered relic of a Stetson that was sweat-stained and curl-brimmed and hip-length Apache moccasins with the stiff, upcurling toe, folded down at the knee. The light brown beard which slurred the outline of a stubborn jaw was bleach-streaked to a lighter hue than his sun-blackened face. His heavy brows were dust-filmed above sardonic, alert amber eyes which never changed, except for a fine deepening of the weather tracks at their outer corners, accenting a squint grown from the habit of scanning distances.

The two men shook hands as soberly and casually as though they had last parted a week, rather than six months, ago. Harley Moffat said then, "Well, I'm damned," standing back with hands on hips, a spare neat man with a benign ruff of sparse graying hair. He eyed Angsman over severely. "Figured you'd show up sporting a charro rig, plenty of braid, and spurs the size of cartwheels."

"Man don't go Mexican from half a year in Sonora," Angsman observed, leaning an arm and hip on the counter. "Besides, I'm not far short of broke, considering."

"Prospected?"

"Around the Madre foothills. Grubstake I bought of you before leaving took the last of my Army pay. That gone, I made do. Jackrabbits, cactus pears, berries, things I won't mention."

"You damned Injun. You look it." Harley Moffat shook his head in wonderment. "And nothing to show for it, eh?"

For answer Angsman drew a nearly flat leather poke from his pocket and laid it on the counter. The sutler picked it up and lightly hefted it, giving an expressive snort. "Six months breaking your back digging and panning, and for what? Damned little dust."

A corner of Angsman's mouth lifted faintly. "Weigh it out."

Moffat carefully spilled the contents of the sack onto a pan of his scales and counterweighted it. "Roughly three ounces, or about seventy-five dollars worth. Anyways, it'll send you off with another grubstake — I reckon?"

Angsman nodded, smiling at his friend's grimace of hopeless disgust. "Hell," Harley Moffat said then, "I gave you up years ago. Gold-grubbing, guiding the soldiers, living with Injuns, batting around the deserts and mountains . . . how many years of it?"

"Eleven."

"An' you're how old? Thirty-five, six?"

"Thirty-one last month."

"Look older. The life, I'd guess." Moffat gave a baffled sigh. "And you'll likely live to be ninety and never sick a day of it . . . you birds always do. Fiddlefooted, no ties, no ownin's, creature comforts an Injun wouldn't envy, and you thrive on it. Plain disgustin'."

"I could open a store. Ought to give me enough worries to put me under the ground inside ten years."

"You could do a sight worse, and the hell with you." The sutler's gaze shuttled above and beyond Angsman's left shoulder. "Oh oh," he said softly. Angsman turned his head enough to see the single rider pacing up the dusty street that passed up from Fort Stambaugh's parade ground between the adobe rows of enlisted men's houses.

"Jack Kincaid," Moffat said. "Been guidin' Lieutenant Storrs on patrol, and it's payday. From the look of him, he had some whisky stashed away. Had, as I say."

Angsman knew Jack Kincaid: a thick bull of a man, composed of brute appetites, who had hunted Indians so long that he rode like one, with toes turned out and heels flailing. He could hold a trail like a hound on the scent; outside of that he was a surly misfit whose brain worked slowly and muddily, a fact which didn't trouble him so long as he could stay drunk, which was nearly always.

Kincaid dismounted at the rail and tied his whey-bellied roan, stood a fuddled moment inspecting Angsman's rawboned and gaunted paint already tied there and the pack horse alongside, then ducked under the tie rail and came onto the porch. He paused hanging to the doorframe, swaying unsteadily and blinking against the dim store interior after leaving the noonday glare. Kincaid's body was blocky and powerful, but lean-shanked; his Ute mother had bequeathed him his straight black hair and high cheekbones and the black bitter eyes, muddy now with liquor and the boiling resentments that surfaced to his mind with it.

He shuffled across to the counter and fell heavily against it, saying thickly, "Wan' a bottle."

"All right, Jack; back in there." Arms folded on the counter, Harley Moffat pointed with his chin toward the swing doors in the partition dividing his store and bar. "Be with you when I've finished here."

Jack Kincaid hammered a meaty fist on the

counter. "Now, li'l man; wan' a bottle now."

"Jack," Moffat said testily but quietly, as though explaining to a child, "you can't just bull over people. Angsman was here before you."

"Let the sonofabitch wait."

Angsman felt the impact of the breed's black hating stare and barely glanced at him, not changing his own negligent pose, saying mildly, "Take care of him, Harley."

"No," Moffat said, his slight frame stiffening, "nobody's bulling over me or my friends in my place. What were we talking about? Your trip?"

"That's about talked out."

"Then we'll talk about the weather. When we settled that, we'll discuss the Indian situation —"

"Don' hear so good, storekeeper," Kincaid rumbled. "When Jack says he wan's a bottle, he don' fool." Abruptly his thick arm swept out and knocked the scales with Angsman's gold spinning from the counter; his other hand leaped across to fist a handful of Harley Moffat's wilted boiled shirt.

Angsman shifted away from the counter, in the same effortless and unbroken movement slashing a rock-hard palm across Kincaid's wrist and breaking his hold, catching the stocky man by the neck. Pivoting to set his weight, he hung Kincaid away. The breed back-pedaled wildly for balance and slammed into a cracker barrel, upsetting it and crashing with it to the floor. He rolled at once to his feet, hand flicking down to a boot-sheath and coming up with six wicked inches of broad-bladed hunting knife. His eyes glinted almost soberly as he moved in on his quarry, this with relief at finding an object on which to vent his stored hatreds.

Angsman began circling out of his reach, baffled but not angry, not wanting to close with the man. You could only pity a man like Jack Kincaid, caught in lonely isolation between two races, too stupid and inflexible to relieve his dilemma except in an occasional drunken, killing rage; he'd had the bad luck to happen along at an infrequent time when the breed's withdrawn surliness had named into open grievance. Yet, too, Angsman felt the pressure of his own unreleased tensions, which built in the toughest loner after months of grueling hardship and solitude. He'd looked forward to a bath and shave and change of clothes, then a few pleasant days of chatting and drinking with old friends. Within a few minutes of hitting the post he was confronted by a drunken, feisty dimwit ready to kill. He felt now a wicked pulse of eagerness that he suppressed; only cold wariness showed in his sidelong retreat. Actually his noiseless mincing shift of body carried him nearer Kincaid, like a big stalking cat.

Forced to a constant clumsy turning to face Angsman's long smooth circling, Kincaid's last shred of caution broke; he lunged bellowing like a bull, blade slashing down in a glittering arc. It didn't come within a foot of Angsman. He'd already leaped aside and was coming in low and fast; his knotted fist met Kincaid's belly beneath the right ribs. It was like connecting with a side of beef.

Kincaid merely gave a coughing grunt and fell back a step, then brought up his blade in a vicious underswing . . . a fluid twist of body and the knife grazed past Angsman's shoulder. Still at close quarters he smashed his lifted forearm across the breed's thick neck muscles. Kincaid heaved forward like an axed steer and Angsman stepped smoothly from his path and pivoted on a heel, fist clubbing Kincaid across the jaw as the man blundered past.

Kincaid wheeled off-balance, sluggish and dazed, to face him. Angsman's stance was already set and he sank his fist into the pit of Kincaid's stomach. It stopped the half-breed cold; his hands dropped to his belly and the knife clattered on the floor. Angsman put his toe against it and skittered it into a corner. Deliberately, he picked his mark and slugged Kincaid in the throat.

Kincaid's knees melted and he slid retching to the floor. Still seething with a residue of anger, Angsman stooped and caught Kincaid by the belt and collar, hauling him bodily to his feet. He rushed him straight at the door, heels digging at the hard-packed clay for momentum, and pulled up suddenly at the threshold, heaving Kincaid's bulky weight up and outward. The half-breed's heels arched over his head in a flailing somersault, and he crashed on his back across the 'dobe porch, impetus bowling him down the steps till he thudded in a dusty sprawl against a tie-rail post.

Breathing a little harder, Angsman watched for a full minute as Kincaid fought to his hands and knees. Harley Moffat tossed out his hat and Kincaid picked it up without looking at them. He dragged himself upright leaning on the cross-rail, elbows hugging his body and his lank greasy hair falling over his eyes. Catching up his reins, he stumbled around the rail to grab his saddle horn blindly; he heaved himself into the leather and swung off down the street.

Watching him go, Angsman felt Harley Moffat's baffled glance. "Funny damned thing. Don't recall seeing you in action before, 'cept for fun. Damn' tiger when you're het up."

Angsman said drily, "Price of survival," and switched the subject. "You mentioned him guiding out a patrol. Trouble?"

"Most always is, from time to time. Nothing like it was, now old Bonito's pulled in his horns. He was the last of the old-time broncho 'Paches, kind the bucks 'ud follow through hell and high water. Your friend Chingo broke reservation again; that's why the colonel had young Storrs on swarry. Chingo and his bunch left a plain trail swingin' southeast; burned a stage station and wiped out a couple settler families on the Gila. Hit and run; wasn't waitin' for the Army to find him, not with only a half-dozen braves, all feisty green youngsters. Anyways the patrol never got a sight of him. Figure he cut 'cross the border, maybe to Geronimo's old stampin' grounds in Sonora. Or could be," Moffat added wryly, "he heard you was down there and is lookin' to roast you head down over a slow fire. . . ."

"He could be, at that." Angsman thought back to his first meeting with the broken-faced, bitter-eyed young war chief . . . three years ago when he'd guided a troop back into the Bailey's Peak country. Straight to a camp of reservation breakaways, a large band of Mimbre warriors and their families, led by El Soldado. It was a rare coup for the Army, that surprise attack on a well-hidden Apache camp in the dead of night. Will Angsman's knowledge of the country and the Apaches was directly responsible for the strategy and success. The Mimbres had rallied — a brief, savage and hopeless defense — and in the blind fracas that followed, Chingo's child-wife and infant son were killed.

That tragic night had branded the war chief's body as well as his brain when, meeting Angsman in hand-to-hand fight, he'd received a defacing wound that had left him hideously scarred. The crippled band was rounded up and returned to reservation, but Chingo, crazed with grief and hatred, had soon broken out, heading up twenty braves to cut a bloody swath across the territory. But Will Angsman tracked him to bay a second time, guiding the troops that cornered him, and wiped out all but a remnant of his followers.

Chingo had guts and brains and heart; a born leader, a generation earlier he might have become another Victorio or Nana or Red Sleeve. But the days of the great war chiefs were long past, and something dark and warped in Chingo's mind, marred by youthful tragedy, caused all but a few of his own people to shun him as a man possessed. After Angsman had twice more led the troops that tracked him down, Chingo's consuming lust to find and kill the white scout had become the blind central goal of his life.

For Angsman there was no personality in their blood feud. Three times he had offered his free services to the Army and tracked Chingo down, because he saw the man's crazed depredations as a menace he'd unintentionally created. He saw Chingo's personal tragedy as part of the great tragedy of the Apache, betrayed and maltreated too many times. No way now to cut off these last flare-ups except by more bloodshed, and Angsman, with the fatalism of a solitary and wilderness-bred man, did his part without futile regret.

Harley Moffat's voice roused him. "Go on in the saloon, pour yourself a drink. Join you when I've cleaned up the dust that damned Kincaid spilled."

Angsman merely nodded because he wanted a drink, in fact, several. He crossed to the swing doors, parted them and entered the musty coolness of the adjoining barroom which smelled pleasantly of sawdust and stale whisky. He got a bottle of Moffat's best from a shelf under the backbar and had barely poured his drink when roistering voices from outside claimed his attention. A dozen thirsty troopers clamored through the swing doors, and he remembered then that Moffat had said it was payday. Angsman knew most of them, greeted them by name, and passed the bottle. When Harley Moffat came in and laid his poke of salvaged gold dust on the oak-plank bar, Angsman said soberly, "Harley, how drunk you reckon we can all get on half of that?"

The troopers laughed and cheered him, but the frugal sutler showed a disgusted scowl. "Much a damned fool as ever, eh? Save out enough of six months' sorry earnings to buy a grubstake an' a new shirt, throw every remainin' cent into drink and cards before strikin' out again. When you goin' to get some sense, Will?"

"Reckon when I've seen the last side of the last hill. . . ."

"I've a mind at times to go see it with you, ye damned tumbleweed," rumbled a deep brogue, and Angsman turned to face the man who had entered, a ruddy-faced trooper built like a squat barrel. They shook hands with mutual pleasure.

Angsman greeted him, "Terence Dahoney, when you end with the service, it'll be the millennium." He added, nodding at the dark patch

17

where chevrons had been on Dahoney's faded blue sleeve, "Demoted again? Major couldn't find any new shavetails for you to field-break?"

"Admittin' nothing," Dahoney answered complacently, " 'ceptin' that B Troop's top noncom was by pure chance the center of an unseemly brawl back of Mr. Moffat's establishment Saturday night last — which the major himsilf, if you please, discovered. I'll have them stripes back inside three months. Meantime I'm secretary-orderly to the major as further punishment, him knowin' I'd rather be swampin' a damned stable."

"Or drinking Mr. Moffat's establishment dry, which project you're in time to help me begin, Terence."

Dahoney shook his head regretfully. "Afraid not, Willis. There's a business a shade more serious afoot, which is why I'm here. From his window the major saw you ride in, this shortly before the two tenderfeet arrived —"

"Tenderfeet?"

"Aye, green as grass, and they're waitin' in the major's office. He sent me to fetch ye before the milk of Erin befuddles your senses. The Old Man is wearin' his best military bark, and I'm thinkin' the matter at hand may be urgent. Ye'd best not keep him waitin'."

CHAPTER TWO

After leaving Angsman's horses at B Stable, he and Terence Dahoney cut between the quartermaster's storehouse and the forage shed and then headed diagonally across Fort Stambaugh's parade ground toward the adobe headquarters building which constituted one side of the east sentry gate. Matching his stride to the brisk, swinging one of the stocky ax-sergeant, Angsman said again, curiously, "Tenderfeet?"

"Aye." Dahoney chewed out his words around the stub of cigar clamped unlit between his bulldog jaws. "A young lady and a gentleman . . . brother and sister, from the look of them; very like the grand toffs I once wheedled for coppers as a guttersnipe on the streets of Boston — from which city I'm thinkin' they hail. The major's askin' for you concerns them; that much I gathered, and no more. . . ." He waved his cigar in a spare semi-circle as they neared the headquarters building. "They're provisioned for a desert trek, wouldn't ye say?"

Angsman nodded briefly, casting an eye over the two saddle horses tied at the weathered rail fronting the building. One bore a sidesaddle. Two pack mules were tied alongside, bulging tarp-covered packs diamond-hitched across their packs.

"Ye'll be at Moffat's later, Willis?" Dahoney asked as they ascended the steps.

"We'll split a bottle there, Terence."

They entered an outer office and circled an endgate to reach a closed door. Dahoney pocketed his cigar stub and rapped a panel with scarred knuckles, bawling briskly, "Mr. Angsman, sor."

Major Philip Marsden opened the door, dismissed Dahoney to his desk with a curt, "All right, trooper," and warmly shook hands with Angsman. "Come in, Will . . . good to see you."

He closed the door behind them, turning toward the man and young woman seated by his desk. "Miss Amberley, Dr. Amberley, may I present Will Angsman, the man I wanted you to meet."

Amberley rose and stepped forward with outstretched hand. He was a slight man in his middle thirties with a thin, sensitive face and gentle blue eyes behind iron-rimmed spectacles. His blond hair was receding above a high, rounded dome of forehead, and his smile, preoccupied and almost absent, was redeemed by a hint of warm shyness. In spite of a mild and scholarly appearance, there was something hard and capable about his wiry frame, this confirmed by his handshake. He wore a wrinkled and travel-stained corduroy suit, the trousers stuffed into

20

high, laced boots, and his flannel shirt was open at the throat.

"Mr. Angsman," he murmured in a precise and pleasant voice. "Major Marsden says that you know the Territory better than any man."

"Except the Apaches."

"Including the Apaches." The major's contradiction was firm in spite of a faint smile. He seated himself in his swivel chair and leaned back, folding his arms across his faded blue blouse. He was a career soldier of fifty, lean of body and face, with a heavy shock of pepper-and-salt hair and a full cavalry mustache. His black eyes were alert and restless, tempered by humor, and there was about him an air of courteous gentility that could harden into steel, as Angsman knew. Stern in his way but not a martinet, Phil Marsden was no garrison soldier and so held Will Angsman's respect.

Angsman glanced now at the young woman seated board-straight in a crude chair by the desk, skirts drawn primly about her ankles. She was about twenty-five or six, he judged, rather thin but trim-figured, not pretty but certainly not plain. Her shining blond hair was parted in the middle and drawn to a chignon at the back of her neck, and she wore a fashionable gray cambric riding habit; a matching wide-brimmed hat sat on her lap. There was a pale delicacy to her smooth face and hands, and unlike her brother — for the identical configuration of their fine-boned features was obvious — she was suffering from the heat. Sweat finely beaded her face and wilted the high close collar of the once-crisp white shirtwaist beneath a close-fitting jacket.

Angsman thought with a faint, dour humor, she's got glassy-eyed from the heat, and she'd fall over in a dead faint before she'd twitch an eyelash. Yet that attitude, hinting at a defiant iron will, aroused his interest enough to let his gaze linger almost boldly on her face. Behind the inner strength reflected there, he felt, with the certainty of wilderness-keened senses, a nature as cold and unbending as ice.

She gave the faintest of cool nods, and Angsman slightly inclined his head, murmuring, "Servant, ma'am," before he put his back to the wall with an angular grace, folding his arms, hat in hand. Amberley motioned toward his chair, but the major said with a humorous lift of eyebrows, "Angsman doesn't use 'em."

Amberley seated himself. The major's swivel chair creaked to a forward tilt of weight as Marsden opened a box of cigars and extended it to Angsman, pausing in mid-motion. "Your permission, ma'am?"

Miss Amberley nodded coolly. Angsman accepted a cigar and Amberley refused, instead taking out a well-blackened pipe which he merely chewed meditatively. Major Marsden lighted Angsman's cigar and his own, then crossed his arms on his scarred desktop.

"Will, these people have their minds set on a

trek into the Sierra Toscos west of the Paisano River. I can't dissuade them. Possibly you can."

Angsman scowled, exhaling a long streamer of smoke. "Bonito's country?"

The colonel nodded with a wry twist of lips.

For thirty years and more, Bonito, the ancient Chiricahua war chief, had been an ever-constant thorn in the side of the Army of the West. He had out-generaled the best officers put in the field against him by never fighting except on ground of his own choosing, with every strategical odd in his favor, a typical Apache stratagem to which Bonito had brought a high polish. When major Apache leaders like Cochise and Mangus Colorado had made their truces with the white invaders, Bonito had warned that the white-eyes' promises were written on wind. Warning unheeded and soon fulfilled.

Only recently, with all except a handful of renegades driven to reservation, Bonito, the Apache who had never stopped fighting, halted his hopeless lifelong war against the whites. Even then he'd refused to surrender or even parley with his hated foes; heading up the last sizable band of non-reservation Chiricahuas, men and women and children, all their gear and animals, he had retreated into the far eastern Sierra Toscos, after serving warning through reservation relatives that should any white-eyed soldiers take the pursuit, they'd fare ill.

Of this there was little danger, as Major Mars-

23

den had drily observed. Standing departmental orders were that no band of the plains tribes, even hostile raiders, were to be molested by the Army patrols, except by direct provocation. A fact of which Bonito was fully aware, for he'd often turned it to shrewd advantage. His message was simply his proudly defiant way of saying he was through fighting. For the old-timers Bonito's action held a trace of nostalgic regret, for it marked the end of something. Henceforth young bucks primed with tiswin and windy stories from their elders might fire up occasionally, as Chingo had again done, but the old days were gone forever. . . .

"As I understand the major," Amberley put in mildly, "the old chief's warning that he'll brook no trespass was directed at any who invade his stronghold with violent intent. However, our own purpose is quite peaceful."

"That so," Angsman murmured.

"Sir," Amberley rejoined sharply, "if I appear green, let me assure you that this isn't wholly the case. I am a professor of archaeology at Harvard University; my specialty is native American civilizations. My field studies have led me to many out-of-the-way places, including Yucatan, southern Mexico, and Peru. I know something of the aboriginal mind; it is my experience that if the natives are treated fairly and honorably, they respond in kind."

"Met any Apaches, professor?"

"No, sir; my field studies have been confined

outside of the United States and its territories, but —"

"Your foreign natives, I'd reckon, had no previous dealings with the white man; the Apaches had a bellyful. Not exactly a hospitable folk, by any odds. Apache's a Zuni word, means enemy."

"Yes, I know."

Because few things irritated Angsman more than a greenhorn's smugness, he said harshly, "Then maybe you ain't green. Maybe you're just a plain damn' fool, Mister."

Miss Amberley stiffened angrily in her chair, and he added coldly, "Your pardon, ma'am." His glance held hard on Amberley's. "Man who puts a shabby premium on his own life may have his reasons. Out here, though, a woman's life means somewhat more."

Amberley's thin tanned face took on a swift ruddy darkening, but it was his sister who spoke first, in a tone the texture of ice: "I — we — are determined, Mr. Angsman. For reasons that you would never understand."

She's determined is what she nearly came out with, ran Angsman's startled thought. Her idea? His gaze shuttled to Amberley for confirmation, found in the hint of wry sheepishness touching his face.

Angsman said with slow bafflement, "Maybe, but I'll give it a try."

"James," she said brittlely.

Amberley breathed a deep sigh, looking from her to Angsman. "Perhaps, sir, you've wrongly concluded that our proposed trek into the Sierra Toscos is in the nature of a scientific expedition; if so, that is my fault through omission. Our only purpose is to find our younger brother, Douglas."

Major Marsden gestured with his cigar. "This is the interesting part, Will. . . . Douglas Amberley's name had a familiar ring — then I remembered. A young fellow by that name came to the fort a year ago. Outfitted at Moffat's store, bought horses, told me he was planning a protracted trip into the eastern Toscos, and could I recommend a guide."

Though this was shortly before Bonito had retreated to that same country, it was ill-reputed by the few prospectors and trappers who'd ventured there as a waterless, barren hellhole. Even the Apaches, who could live on ground mesquite beans and cactus fruit, if necessary, had generally shunned it. Naturally, the major said, he'd tried to dissuade the young man; he wasn't over twenty-one, obviously Eastern and inexperienced. But the boy was adamant, and reluctantly the major had acquired for him the best guide available at the time, old Caleb Tree.

Tree was one of the last of the mountain men, crowding seventy now, irascible and mean and probably unscrupulous, but he knew the Apaches and the country as few white men did; and for enough money he'd undertake anything. Young Amberley had met his price without hesitation, and they'd struck west from Fort Stambaugh, equipped and provisioned for a lengthy sojourn in the wilds. The major could only assume they'd met with an accident — or fallen victim to Bonito's warriors when they made their unexpected withdrawal into the Toscos three months later.

"Your brother," the major concluded, "was absolutely silent about his purpose, Dr. Amberley. I hope you'll be more explicit. What in the devil was he after?"

Amberley hesitated. "Secrecy is hardly of importance now, of course. . . . My brother had chosen my own profession, archaeology, as his life's work. Only —" Again Amberley hesitated with a brief glance at his sister, apparently weighing his words — "Douglas was more restless than I. After three years of study at Harvard, he quit and went West. Two years earlier, at nineteen, he'd accompanied me to Mexico, to study the Toltec-Aztec ruins near Vera Cruz, an experience that had deeply fired his imagination. For months after he'd left Boston, we received no word — until a letter arrived, posted from Santa Fe. . . ."

The letter had obviously been penned in high excitement. Douglas told how he'd toured the old Spanish missions of the southwest, poring exhaustively through their archives, examining hundreds of forgotten documents, for a shred of truth in the early Spaniards' belief that the puissant Aztecs, at the height of their power in Mexico, had established northern colonies in Arizona or New Mexico. An idea refuted by Prescott and other authorities, it had come to obsess Douglas.

He'd found nothing to confirm the theory, and was further discouraged by the present refusal of the Catholic Church to open certain stores of early Spanish records, secreted in missions and monasteries, to investigators. And so his youthful and restless curiosity was diverted by an unexpected discovery at a little mission in a Pueblo village outside of Santa Fe. Here the Franciscan fathers had been most co-operative, and in their archives he'd uncovered an old manuscript penned here more than two centuries before by a Castilian grandee, Don Pedro de Obregon, then buried away to gather dust.

Obregon had been an exacting scholar as well as gentleman adventurer, and his fine flowing script offered easy translation. His account was of a journey that he and other soldiers-of-fortune had made in 1672, in an effort to find a trace of the legendary Cibola and its treasures the golden lure which had first brought Coronado and his successors to this land.

Striking southwest from Santa Fe on the trail of one illusive but persistent rumor, Obregon and his well-equipped party of nine Spaniards and a score of Indians had crossed desert and mesa for weeks till in rugged country they struck a great mountain pass and swung eastward to follow it out. For days they moved deeper into the barren and desolate range. With their water running dangerously low and most of them ready to backtrail, they came to a stream of clear water.

A little farther on, beneath the towering escarpment of a giant mesa, they found an incredibly wealthy vein of high-grade gold.

Their former goal utterly forgotten in this dazzling find, Obregon and his party drove their Indians mercilessly to erect a small stone fort against the bands of roaming *Querechos,* as the Spaniards had dubbed the Apaches. Then they began tunneling into the mountain from the rear of their fortress, tearing out great gold-rich chunks of ore, while a smelter was built close by. So rich was the vein that within a short time they had as much as they could pack out. Lacking molds, they poured the melted metal into improvised hide tubes to cool into heavy bars, loading these onto their sturdy Moorish ponies till the poor beasts staggered beneath the weight.

But the Querechos, by now gathering to one sizable band, were waiting unseen above the pass. Don Pedro de Obregon's party had no sooner abandoned their fort and struck upcanyon than the Querechos had surrounded and cut them off. The first volley of arrows had killed two Spaniards and four Indians; the remaining Indians fled in panic and were slaughtered like quail on the run. The surviving Spaniards kept the enemy temporarily at bay with their arquebuses, whose noise and smoke demoralized the surprised savages more than the whistling balls.

Slowly the Spaniards fell back to a trail which mounted the flanking pass wall to a high cave mouth. Because they refused to abandon their gold-laden animals, driving the terrified beasts up the narrow trail, two more Spaniards died before the survivors achieved the cave. From this position they easily defended the single narrow trail, though now the Querechos simply camped below for a patient siege.

They found water in the honeycombing of the caves, but their provisions, already depleted, soon ran out. A fifth man died in a quarrel over the last strip of dried meat. They killed their ponies for food, but the meat quickly spoiled. In desperation three of the remaining four decided on a break by night. The last man, Don Pedro de Obregon, listened in the darkness to their descent . . . heard them die at the hands of the waiting enemy.

A week later Don Pedro himself, nearly out of his mind with privation and shattered nerves, left the caves by full daylight and started the long trek back to Santa Fe. The Querechos, evidently believing this babbling survivor to be deranged, let him go. Of the nightmarish days that followed the Don had little memory. Somehow he'd crossed miles of mountain and desert wilderness to stagger, more dead than alive, into a village of Christianized Pueblos. These friendly natives bore him on by travois to Santa Fe and left him in the hands of the padres at the little mission of Tesque.

Rest and care brought Obregon gradually back to his senses. Broken in mind and body by his harrowing adventure, he didn't live out the year.

On his deathbed he penned an account of the aborted mission; he set it down at the urging of his confessor, Father Garcia, to whom he had unburdened his venial conduct.

Young Douglas Amberley made the shrewd guess that the Franciscan Garcia had Don Pedro write his narrative, then himself withheld it from colonial representatives of the Spanish crown, with the intention of somehow channeling the wealth waiting in those far mountains into the coffers of the Church — for Obregon had included a detailed map and directions. Yet for unknown reasons the parchment manuscript lay buried for two centuries among other forgotten records.

Quietly, James Amberley now drew a folded paper from his pocket and handed it to Angsman. "There is the copy of Obregon's chart which Douglas sent me, together with description and directions translated from the Spanish."

Angsman unfolded the map and briefly scanned its painstakingly penciled lines and printed script, quickly identifying the meandering course of the Paisano River and other prominent landmarks. Obregon had other names for these, but had placed them with scrupulous accuracy. Was the half of the *derrotero* that charted the little-known country to the east of the river equally true? He felt irritation at his own stirring interest . . . treasure maps and lurid legends foisted off on greenhorns were a dime a dozen.

31

Curiously studying the chart, he noted a heavily marked cross underscored with the only words not rendered from the Spanish. *"Muro del Sangre,"* he murmured. "The Wall of Blood."

"That would be the location of the mine, according to the directions," Amberley interjected. "Cryptic bit of picturesque whimsy, eh? Touch of enigmatic poetry within the old boy's clear and factual prose. Seems to be descriptive, but I can't unravel its significance. Neither could Doug."

Angsman handed back the paper. "Did your brother say he intended findin' the mine?"

Amberley nodded soberly. "Starting from the nearest outpost — Fort Stambaugh. I wrote him promptly, advising against undertaking so hazardous a project alone in his inexperience. Suggested that he wait for me in Contentionville, where we could outfit and organize an expedition properly. Either he didn't receive the letter or, what's more likely, chose to ignore it. His next communication, and his last, was mailed from this fort — a brief hasty note. If he didn't return, his ownings were to be equally divided between his sister and me. That was all.

"I wanted to come West at once, but the Harvard trustees, academically conservative gentlemen, would not grant me a leave of absence, though a sabbatical leave was pending. I pointed out that Don Pedro's mine should prove an eminent archaeological find. They pooh-poohed the notion; my brother was irresponsible, as his

32

quitting school demonstrated, and my judgment was overbalanced by concern. I pointed out that the conditions of Douglas' finding the Obregon manuscript certainly indicated its authenticity, while Don Pedro, penning it on his deathbed, would have been in a passion to reveal the truth. Vain argument. It wasn't till now that my sabbatical leave came up — and Judith and I left as soon as possible."

Amberley's explanation of why he'd let a year drag by after his brother's last message bore a false ring in its painstaking detail; it occurred to Angsman that the man might be covering a sense of guilt. But he said nothing.

Major Marsden leaned intently forward now, lacing his fingers together on his desktop. "Well, Will — what's your verdict? You know the Toscos."

Angsman scowled at his cigar. "Not that part of it, Phil, not Bonito's country. Prospected west of the Paisano River, that's all." He glanced abruptly at the Amberleys, laying down his words hard and flat. "Might have been a chance of finding your brother alive nine, ten months ago. Not a year later, and not with the Chiricahuas dug in back there. You waited too long. My advice, get back to Boston, forget about it."

He said it with intentional brutality, hoping to drive a wedge of sense through this wall of greenhorn ignorance. But Judith Amberley said with no lessening of her inflexible coldness, "Mr.

33

Angsman, I have a suggestion."

"Ma'am?"

"You have stated by inference that we are rash and misguided fools, ignorant of the country and its dangers. As bears on our ignorance, your surmise is accurate. We would be helpless as children. You would not be. Therefore . . . will you be our guide?"

Her bluntness disconcerted Angsman, as he guessed she'd intended it should, and now he shifted his shoulders uncomfortably. "No, ma'am; I have not lived this long by being a purple fool."

Her face pinkened beneath its pale gloss, but her tone held even: "I believe that I can offer a reason that should outweigh any objection."

"Yes'm."

"Money," she said laconically and flatly. "I will give you a draft on our bank for the sum you name, in advance of our leaving."

"No, ma'am," Angsman said quietly, stubbornly. "This is a fool thing you propose, and I will not be party to helping two people throw away their lives for no reason."

"I think, sir, that you are a coward."

Angsman pushed away from the wall and moved soundlessly to the door, pausing to say, "That is your privilege," and then with a soft, sardonic, "Servant, ma'am," he was gone.

CHAPTER THREE

Following the awkward silence after the door closed behind Angsman, Major Marsden said courteously, but obviously supressing his anger, "I am trying to understand you, Miss Amberley."

"Judith, there was no call to pointedly insult the man!" James Amberley half-rose, his face deeply flushed. "Major, I must apologize —"

The major brushed aside his words with a curt, "Perhaps later, Dr. Amberley; I'd not approach Angsman now. He may well be in a mood to smash your jaw."

"No doubt," Judith Amberley said. "The man is a rude, unshaven boor. I see no reason to suppose him infallible — nor did I like his attitude or choice of words. I am sorry, Major, but that is my exact impression — and I am accustomed to speaking my mind exactly."

"I at least respect your candor," the major said slowly. "Will was a little rough. But he is never irresponsible; I believe that his harshness was intended to dissuade you from what he summed up in no uncertain terms, and quite accurately." His pleasant courtesy restored now, he added, "Obviously this journey has been a trying one for you, Miss Amberley. . . ."

She nodded, a faint concern in her cool smile, and now her brother studied her with genuine concern, seeing her face pale and drawn beneath a dew of perspiration. He knew her steel-willed checkrein on any display of feeling or pain, yet her cool, uncomplaining poise till now had been so convincing he'd forgotten that she was a soft and gently bred Eastern woman.

Marsden continued gravely, "My wife and I would be honored to have you both as overnight guests."

"We couldn't think of putting you to all that bother, Major," Judith said aloofly. Amberley inwardly damned her stiff-necked pride; too often she carried it beyond good sense.

But Marsden was convincingly insistent. The commandant's house had two large spare rooms ready for occupancy; his wife's home ties were in Boston, and she would be eager for news. Anyway, the major added smiling, it would do them both good to sleep on their illusions. His warm argument partly melted Judith's frosty reserve, and she managed a wan smile of agreement.

The commandant's house lay at the end of Officer's Row, and there Marsden introduced his wife, a plump and motherly woman who clucked solicitously over Judith and afterward hurried her off to a room where she might clean up and rest.

"I must see to our horses, Major," Amberley said. "And then, if you've a few minutes to spare,

I hope you'll join me in a drink at the post trader's bar."

The major was agreeable, and they returned to the headquarters building where Marsden called out Trooper Dahoney and told him to take the Amberleys' saddle and pack animals to B Stable and see that they were unloaded and cared for. As Dahoney saluted and turned to untie the horses, the major ran an approving eye over them.

"You're a keen judge of horseflesh, I see, Doctor, a man wants animals with plenty of bottom for the desert."

"Yes . . . we outfitted just across the river from the fort, at Contentionville," Amberley explained as they swung into step, headed for the sutler's. "I'm no stranger to wilderness jaunts. With Judith — it's another matter."

"She is a strong-minded woman, your sister," Marsden mused aloud, "but plainly unfit for the rigors of what you've planned." He hesitated. "I don't question her intelligence, but I must admit that her insistence on this dangerous and hopeless mission, more particularly her insistence on personally undertaking it, puzzles me. Your younger brother, after all, was a grown man . . . tackled his venture of his own will. She must think a great deal of him."

"Why," Amberley said absently, "you might call it an act of atonement, Major."

Realizing that he'd encroached on a highly personal matter, Marsden partly veered the subject. "I should say," he stated almost curtly, "that as the family head, you should assert your views over and above hers. She certainly can't carry the thing further without you. You'll pardon my bluntness, Doctor; I think the situation warrants it. That young lady must be brought to her senses."

Amberley smiled thinly. "You don't know my sister, sir. . . ."

As they neared the sutler's, the swing doors of the saloon burst open and Will Angsman and a half-dozen troopers, loud with drink and argument, filed out, two of them with arms slung around Angsman's shoulders. All seven were out of sight between two buildings by the time Amberley and the major had reached the porch.

"What was that about?" asked the mystified Easterner.

"Let's find out," the major said, his eyes twinkling.

Inside the barroom, now deserted except for the sutler, Amberley was introduced to Harley Moffat, and then Marsden said: "What was the ruckus, Mr. Moffat?"

"Ah, Angsman's goin' to show the boys some Injun wrestlin' throws. Says if he can't flatten each in turn inside a minute, he'll pay for all the drinks. Reckon they'll conduct the show over behind the stables." Harley Moffat clucked his tongue resignedly.

A puckish smile touched the major's lips. "Suppose I'll have to break that up, but no hurry.

We'll have a drink, Mr. Moffat, and you'll join us."

"By all means," Amberley said, smiling at the commandant's flexible disciplinary line; it left a broad latitude for release from the tensions, privations, and monotony of frontier duty.

The major now briefly mentioned Amberley's intended search for his brother, and Harley Moffat reinforced the other pessimistic reactions. "If you're set in your mind, sir, damn' pity you couldn't get Angsman as guide. If anyone could take you into hostile territory and out alive, that's the man. Otherwise. . . ." Moffat clucked sadly.

Amberley nodded absently, curiously wondering about the man. All these Western men were hard and weather-scoured, yet they all seemed almost pale and soft compared to Will Angsman. Definitely a Southerner from his speech . . . or had been. It was difficult to tell much else; he guessed that even with his friends the man would be almost stoically reserved, blunt and brief-spoken. Yet he plainly had friends, and not only among the rough troopers. Though the major must be worlds apart from Angsman — for it was a far cry from the rigid military echelons to Angsman's hard-bitten independence — Marsden plainly liked the man. He seemed utterly complete and self-sufficient; you could feel it in him, along with the incredible alertness and animal vitality in repose.

There came an unsteady shuffle of boots across the porch, and the major, glancing across the swing doors, murmured wryly, "I see that Mr. Kincaid is losing no time in disposing of his pay."

Harley Moffat swore softly. "Will Angsman threw him out once today — after he picked a fight." He raised his voice sharply as a thick-set, Indian-looking man blundered through the doors. "Jack, if you drink here, you mind your manners now."

Jack Kincaid stood in the center of the room swaying unsteadily, his bloodshot eyes moving almost furtively over the three men. He wiped his nose on his knuckles and lurched heavily to the other end of the bar. "Jus' gimme bottle," he muttered surlily.

Moffat silently set a glass and full whisky bottle in front of him. Kincaid slapped some coins on the bar, sloshed his glass full and settled down to morose, steady drinking. Amberley gave him a wondering regard, then swallowed his own drink.

As he and Major Marsden left the barroom, pausing on the porch, a group of four riders swung up the street. A strangely assorted quartet, Amberley saw as they drew near, but alike in their tacky civilian clothes, their worn, dusty and weathered appearance.

"These gentlemen seem to have ridden long and hard —"

"They always do." Marsden's reply was taut and harsh. "You have the dubious honor of viewing the worst gang of blackguards and cutthroats the border country has produced. Armand Charbonneau and his precious coterie. Damn — I'd hoped he'd stay in Mexico. . . ."

As he spoke the major was moving off the porch, confronting the four as they reined to a dusty halt. The leader swung off his rawboned sorrel in a long agile movement that reminded Amberley of a snake uncoiling . . . odd in a man so gaunt and towering. He was about forty, with a long axblade of a face darkened by wind and sun. His cocksure blandness was relieved by a great beak of a nose and a trim black mustache, a jutting jaw slurred by a ragged spade beard. His pale eyes were a flashing and luminous green, almost startling against his dark complexion. His long black hair was queued at the side, hanging past his collar. He wore a battered sombrero, a discolored and greasy deerhide coat, and frayed tight butternut pants stuffed into high jackboots. A twisted cheroot projected jauntily from a corner of his chalky smile.

He advanced with a gliding ease, throwing his arms wide, booming, "Ah, *mon ami* the major. 'Ow are you, my fran'?"

Marsden ignored the outstretched hand, his tone saber-keen: "This post is off-limits to you, Charbonneau. Has been since you smuggled that rotgut to reservation Chiricahuas last year."

Armand Charbonneau's brows rose in a deeply pained look; he spread his open palm against his chest. "You do not mean Armand, my fran'? Oh no, it is mistake, eh? I thought you 'ave hear bettair by this time. Armand nevair do such thing —"

"Not so anyone can prove it," Marsden cut in. "One of these days your cleverness will trip you up for fair — and I hope you're on this side of the big river when it happens. I'd hate to let the Mexican army have the pleasure of standing you against a wall." He paused, struck by a thought. "How the hell did you get past the sentry?"

"Ah, ha. If the major do not want his great fran' inside his so fine fort, he should not post the gate with green recruit, eh?" Charbonneau's broad shoulders shook with noiseless mirth. "I tal' him the major send for Armand and his fran's for the guiding. Is great joke, *non?*"

"Damn your gall, Charbonneau!" The major dashed his cigar to the hard-packed ground. "All right. Now you're here, have your drink. But you'd dawn' well better be gone inside the hour!"

There was a cavalier and satirical elegance to Charbonneau's mocking bow. "*Merci,* my fran'. Come, *mes amis;* we toast Armand's good fran' the major in M'sieu Moffat's bad whisky. Come!"

The other three dismounted and silently followed the leader through the swing doors. Amberley, staring after them in fascination, swung to Major Marsden. "Why, Major, this man is fabulous! — a latter-day buccaneer to the hilt. Why don't you go on alone, sir; I'd like to stay a while. . . ."

"Fabulous," Marsden snorted quietly, dourly. "You tenderfeet and your Wild West. . . . All right, Doctor — but a word of caution. Just watch them, and no more. Under his dash and color, your swashbuckling friend is a snake."

With a curt nod, he strode away, cutting out of sight between the buildings where Angsman and the troopers had gone. Then Amberley jerked about, startled, as the swing doors parted suddenly and the dark, squat Kincaid leaped out backward onto the porch, crouched and poised, a long wicked knife in his palm. One of Charbonneau's men lunged out, his fists raised. He was a giant coal-black Negro whose chest and shoulders swelled against his soiled shirt with the latent power of a young bull.

" 'Tol you next time we met I'd slit your gizzard, Armbuster," Kincaid hissed.

"That's the secon' time jus' now you call me Armbuster," the Negro rumbled, lumbering about in an effort to front the other. "You know my name's Ambruster. I'm gwine break you back fo' that, po' breed trash —"

"Turk!"

Charbonneau stood in the doorway, his voice cracking like a whip. "You want to get us all in the post guardhouse, eh? The major, he say drink, not fight. An' you, Jack, when 'ave we been bad fran's, eh? I think now you shake hands, we all drink on it."

Kincaid sullenly lowered the knife, rocking back on his heels. "I'll drink with you, Armand.

43

But I don't shake hands with no nigger."

A rumble rose from Ambruster's cavernous chest.

Charbonneau flicked the ash from his cheroot. "Turk, get inside now. Armand does not fool. Inside!"

Suddenly the Negro laughed sheepishly, and it transformed his thick brutal face. Amberley had the startled thought, Why, the man's neither slow nor stupid — if this isn't the strangest. . . .

Ambruster went in past Charbonneau, who now stepped out to slap Kincaid smartly on the shoulder. "Come on now, Jack." He poked Kincaid playfully in the ribs and flashed his white streak of a smile. "Get in there and drink."

Kincaid's surly face broke in a reluctant grin; he followed Ambruster. Charbonneau was about to swing after him when his curious gaze found Amberley staring open-mouthed.

"Beg pardon. Didn't mean to stare. But, by George, sir — yours is an iron hand."

For a moment Charbonneau seemed puzzled, then he gave an explosive laugh. "Merci, Mistair Dude. Ah, maybe you have a drink with Armand too? Eh?"

"Why — yes, thank you."

Charbonneau shouldered up to the bar between two of his men. "These *bon amis* are Will-John Staples and Ramon Uvaldes. Mistair — ?"

"Amberley, James Amberley."

Will-John Staples shook hands readily, and his

palm was thick and calloused. He was a short, barrel-chested young man in his early twenties with a round, mild face and eyes of a deep and dreamy brown. A tow cowlick hung over his ruddy forehead, he continually, absently tossed it back in a way that reminded Amberley of a stolid bull head-tossing at an annoying horsefly. He had the appearance of a thick-headed farmboy, seeming badly, out of place with this hard-bitten trio.

Uvaldes was a lean villainous-looking man with a great knife scar cutting transversely across a narrow coffee-brown face. Without turning from the bar, he flicked a black lightning stare over Amberley and then looked away.

Charbonneau cocked an elbow on the bar and tugged at his ear, facing Amberley with an appraising grin. "M'sieu, you are a gentleman, this is plain. Armand Charbonneau, who come of fine Creole family, does not mistake such things. Hah. Gentleman drink apart, *hein?* Come."

He flipped a bottle into one sinewy hand, scooped up two glasses with the other as Harley Moffat set them out, then jerked his head toward a round deal table in the corner. With half-amused curiosity Amberley followed him, taking the stool which Charbonneau indicated with a sweep of his hand. The air of someone at once raffish and dashing, engaging and knavish, that clung to him fascinated the Easterner. Maybe I'm the toad that the snake has mesmerized, he thought amusedly.

Charbonneau poured their drinks. "To the jade called fortune, M'sieu; may she smile on us both." They drank, and Charbonneau grew voluble and expansive; obviously his favorite topic was himself. With gestures as eloquent as his colorful speech, he sketched a past of scandalous rascality.

"Such are the sad misdemeanairs of the black sheep scion of high-placed N'Orleans family, one in whose mouth the silvair spoon turn to tarnish," he concluded, grinning, and then his green eyes pronged abruptly against Amberley's. "And now, M'sieu, what of you? You are no book-bound scholair merely, *n'est-ce pas?*"

"My work has entailed considerable travel," Amberley admitted modestly.

"Ha! This I knew." He refilled the Easterner's glass for the third time. "Tell me of your work, m'sieu. . . ."

Afterward Amberley was never certain how it had come about, but there was Charbonneau with Douglas' map spread out on the table before him, asking penetrating and detailed questions in the most casually friendly manner.

Amberley tried to sort out coherent replies; his tongue seemed thick, and the room rolled like a ship's deck whenever he moved his eyes. He'd never had much stomach for liquor, even in his slightly rowdy undergraduate days, and he thought worriedly, Damned pleasant, chatting with this frontier chevalier, but I must stop drinking now. Judith will be furious. . . .

He knit his brows befuddledly. "Wha' d'you say jus' then, Armand?"

"I say, smart boy with all that learning, like your brothair — he wouldn' kite off into the desert on the wild goose hunt, professair, eh?"

"Uh . . . yes, quite so."

"You need anothair drink, *mon ami.*"

"No. Uh-uh. Mus' insist. Quite enough."

"We 'ave not drink to friendship." Overriding Amberley's mild protest, Charbonneau poured another round. He raised his glass with eyes emerald-hard and glinting above its rim. "Doctair, I think we do each othair some good. You listen now to Armand, eh?"

CHAPTER FOUR

Angsman woke with a bad taste in his mouth. He rolled onto his back and inched to a sitting position in the hay, gently massaging his pounding head, wincing as the early sunlight seeping into the stable loft dislodged savage splinters behind his eyes. He found his crumpled hat beside him in the straw and clamped it on. As he climbed laboriously to his feet, holding a wall for support, he gave a ragged shudder and breathed gingerly against his bruised ribs where an over-sportive trooper had dropped on him with both knees during their mock brawl.

Bleakly he stared out the loading window of the loft, finding the morning tasteless and drab. Maybe it was only the dismal reaction of a hangover, yet Angsman couldn't recall feeling such a gray emptiness as filled him this morning. Thirty-one years of living . . . and nothing to show for it but his gun, saddle, scars, and empty pockets.

Yet these things had always been enough, along with the freedom and the desert life and the many friends he rarely saw. The pure freedom he wanted made necessary the shunning of any strong human ties. Maybe he was rimming a crucial summit in his life and seeing the other side desolate and aimless. . . .

The hell with it.

He was letting his physical misery affect his mood, that was all; a bath and a solid meal would set him up again. Even so, breathing shallowly against his bruises and hangover as he moved to the loft traphole and descended the ladder, he resolved to go easier; he was no longer the green and resilient boy he'd been.

Down in the runway Angsman exchanged amiable insults with the stable sergeant while he rummaged through the pack of supplies for which he'd paid Harley Moffat the last of his dust and which he'd left in an empty stall. He dug out the stiff new shirt and trousers and headed for Officer's Row, answering casually to greetings of officers and enlisted men alike.

Though he'd slept through reveille and the sun was already high and strong in the brassy sky, the day was young. Breathing deeply of the air and sunlight and dust, Angsman felt more his usual self, even felt a mild pleasure on briefly reviewing his future plans. He had none in particular: loaf around the fort a day or so, cross over to Contentionville and renew some acquaintances, then strike out again. Probably north this time; it didn't really matter.

A scowl knitted his brows as his mind flicked back to yesterday in Marsden's office. He felt an obscure guilt at his indifferent judgment of those greenhorns. No concern of his, yet he hoped the Amberleys might now have the sense to go back where they belonged. On reflection, he couldn't blame the woman for countering his rudeness with an acrid insult of her own; no doubt her ultimate judgment of him was that he was a shiftless, useless frontier tramp. Which is close enough, he thought with a wry grin, and dismissed the incident from his thoughts.

Angsman tramped around the long building that housed the bachelor officers' quarters to the bathhouse at its rear. Five minutes later, standing under the shower and soaping his chest and shoulders, he glanced around as the door opened, seeing Terence Dahoney's broad bulk filling the doorway.

"I'm thinkin' that of us two, you're the wiser," Dahoney commented phlegmatically. "Today's that much a scorcher, I'd like to tell the major fie on his paperwork and the damned Army too, and join ye." He glanced over Angsman's lean white body with its startling contrast of deeply weathered face and neck and hands, and added, "That's why I don't. Look at the likes of you, ganted up like a deer-huntin' dog. The service at the least fills a man's belly."

"You've got pretty soft, Terence," Angsman observed. He waited for Dahoney's derisive snort, then grinned, "If you didn't come for a bath . . . ?"

"The major sent me to find you, an' Trooper Wilcox saw you headin' for here."

"Now what the hell?" Angsman asked with a mild irritation.

"I dunno, Willis. Only that he's in higher dudgeon than yesterday. Ye'd best lose no time. . . ."

Ten minutes later Angsman walked into the commandant's office, nodded to Major Marsden's grim and unsmiling greeting, and took his position against the wall, stirring his shoulders uncomfortably against the scratchy newness of his crease-stiff shirt and trousers, having discarded his other ragged clothes.

Marsden said flatly and without preliminary, "They did it. Kited off into the desert without a by-your-leave."

"The Amberleys, eh?"

The major stood, paced an angry circle of the desk and halted facing him. "Yes, dammit — stole off at first dawn before either Elsa or I were awake." He sighed and scrubbed his jaw with the flat of his palm, a gesture of weary disgust. "Let me start at the beginning. I invited the Amberleys to stay the night at our place. Then he and I went to the sutler's for a drink. As we were leaving, Armand Charbonneau and his gang of tough nuts rode in —"

"Charbonneau. . . ." Angsman scowled. "Thought he'd have the sense to stay clear of Stambaugh after I uncovered his whisky-peddling last year. Didn't he head for Mexico?"

"He did, and stayed long enough to let the event cool. No case that'd hold water, and he knew it. Came riding in bold as brass, bluffed his way past the sentry. I told him to have his drink and clear out. Dr. Amberley was taken with the dawned blackguard, stayed to size Charbonneau up. I'd warned the fool not to get cozy with Charbonneau, but — I got the rest of the story from Harley Moffat this morning."

The sutler had noticed that the professor was holding his liquor badly, and that the rascally Creole obviously had his nose to the wind and was straining at the leash. Busy serving drinks to Charbonneau's thirsty crew, Moffat had paid no great attention to the pair's low-voiced conversation, lost in the general hubbub. Then Charbonneau had abruptly called his pack to heel and they'd ridden away. Jack Kincaid had left with them which had struck Moffat as odd, there being bad blood between the half-breed and Turk Ambruster, Charbonneau's right-hand man. Then the professor, weaving badly but navigating on his own, had left.

At the major's house, his wife had greeted Amberley pleasantly, without comment on his condition, and had shown him to his room. Judith Amberley was napping at the time. Later the major and his wife had enjoyed a tolerant chuckle over the incident, both agreeing to say nothing to the strait-laced Miss Amberley about her brother's unseemly behavior.

Later, as the Marsdens were retiring, they heard the Amberleys conversing in low tones in the sister's room. James Amberley had apparently slept off his liquor, and now, the major guessed, he and Judith were discussing their future plans. His first alarm hadn't come till this morning when Elsa went to wake the Amberleys for breakfast and found both of them gone.

Marsden had hurried to the stables, there to learn from the stable sergeant that the two Easterners had claimed their horses and pack gear an hour before reveille. Next the colonel had checked with the night sentry at the east gate, learning that the Amberleys had left the fort at first light and headed due east across the flats. Afterward, idly following their progress from the wall, the sentry had seen five horsemen, too distant to identify, canter over a low range of dunes and meet the Amberleys. The seven of them had ridden on together. Though curious, the sentry had made nothing of the incident, nor thought it worth reporting at the time. Finally on a hunch, the major had talked to Harley Moffat, finding his worst fears verified.

Angsman said softly, "Charbonneau, eh?"

"Who else? Amberley innocently mentioned his brother's mission, and at the mention of gold, Charbonneau became a wolf on the scent. In Amberley's state, he'd have needed little persuasion to fall in with our charming rogue's suggestion that he and his crew were just the men to guide them into the Sierra Toscos and bring them out alive. . . ."

Angsman rubbed his chin reflectively. "And he'd figure his past renegade dealings with

'Paches, some hostile, would get him past Bonito. Plenty risk even so, but the stakes'd be
worth it."

"Yes, exactly; the point is those poor fools are
lambs ripe for the shearing — I should say
slaughter, with that wolf-pack."

"Send a detail to bring 'em back."

The major snorted impatiently. "You know
how the settlers resent the military, though our
only purpose here is to protect them. In extreme
cases when we've had to declare martial law, the
stink invariably carries clear to Washington. War
Department sends us strict orders to handle ci-
vilians with kid gloves. What in hell can I do?
Hogtie our two lambs and bring them back at
bayonet point? For unless I'm mistaken, you
couldn't sway that Amberley girl otherwise. Has
a mind like a steel trap — dominates her brother,
if you noticed — and has some almighty intense
reason to go ahead with this damnfool search,
something beyond ordinary family affection."
The major paused deliberately. "The point is,
it's a free country, person can come or go at
their whim. I work for that country; my hands
are tied. Yours aren't."

"Wondered when you'd get to that."

"Will you do it?"

Angsman nodded wearily. "I'll bring your
lambs back. Can't promise all the fleece'll be
intact."

"Good," Phil Marsden said briskly. "Of
course, the assignment's wholly unofficial, and

54

this conversation never took place. You'll handle it as you think best . . . and accordingly, you're not merely on your own — the full responsibility for your action is on your head. Understood?"

"Pretty clear buck-passing, Phil."

"Sorry, Will. You know I'm strapped."

"Sure. I'll want one man, a good one."

"How about Mexican Tom?"

"The best, when he's sober. Where in hell is Tom?"

"Still on our guide payroll, and his wife still takes in laundry for the enlisted men. Tom, I regret to say, got drunk the other night and started shooting at the sky. Roused the whole post — thought it was a new uprising. To make a long story short, he's in the guardhouse serving a thirty-day sentence."

Angsman chuckled. "Same old Tomas. . . ."

Marsden reached down his battered campaign hat and clamped it on. "Let's get him out."

Angling across the parade grounds and approaching the guardhouse, they heard the strains of a discordant but lively harmonica playing *La Cucaracha* drifting from the single barred window. The major spoke to the trooper on guard, who opened the barred door. Angsman followed the major inside, ducking his tall frame through the low doorway.

Tomas Ramirez was sprawled on his back across a bunk, one leg cocked up and the other trailing on the floor, his eyes closed. He tapped the harmonica on his wrist, pocketed it, and opened a black sparkling eye. He wasn't much past twenty, a squat brown gnome of a young man with a long lantern jaw which sagged in a lazy grin; he idly lifted a hand without otherwise stirring.

"*Buenas dias,* Willie. Heard you was on the post. Hey, you come to get Tomas out? We catch big drunk, eh?"

"You catch nothing from me but hell, Tomas."

Mexican Tom yawned and sat up, running one hand through his short curly hair, reached the other inside his cotton shirt and scratched his ribs. Angsman detected the wicked glint in his eye and was ready when Tom made a sudden grab at his wrist. Angsman sidestepped, grabbed his wrist and threw him face down across the bunk with a knee in his back. Both of them were laughing when Angsman released him and Tom bounded to his feet to pump his hand.

"You damned big kid," Angsman growled amiably. "When you going to grow up?"

"Hell, amigo, I got a whole life for that. Hey, you pretty fit for an old man. Come on, we catch that drink."

"Not so fast, Ramirez," the major said curtly. "I'm releasing you on conditions — one of which is, no drinking."

"Sure, big chief. It's what you say. Even so, by damn, is good to see you, Willie."

As they stepped outside, Marsden said, "You're under Angsman's orders, Tom. He'll explain the situation. . . ." He extended his hand then, and Angsman took it. "Will, Miss Amberley should give you more trouble than Charbonneau. Go careful, and luck to you."

Angsman and Mexican Tom moved off toward the married enlisted men's row, Angsman quietly filling in the situation. Ramirez nodded in ready agreement. "I'm with you. Been honin' for excitement, and they ain't none to be had in this pesthole. Soon's I'm outfitted and say *adios* to my woman, we make the dust."

At the little Ramirez adobe at the far end of the row, Mexican Tom assembled his gear while his pretty wife flailed him with a furious tongue. "*Madre de Dios,* before you are out of the *calabozo* almost, you ride off. . . . Ongsman, can you no leave my *bellaco* of a hosband with me a while, *por favor?* I will give him such a crack on the head. . . ."

"Sorry, Lupe. I need him now." Angsman's quick eye traced a furtive movement. "Tomas, what'd you slip in that saddlebag?"

"Oh, nothing, amigo."

Angsman's hand dipped into the saddlebag and came up with a full pint of whisky. "None of that," he said roughly, and handed the bottle to Lupe. "Not this trip. I mean it, Tomas."

Mexican Tom spread his hands in abject mockery. "I am jus' one no-good bom, amigo." To which Lupe added her shrill, angry agreement.

They rode steadily across the mesquite-laced

57

flats until, toward late afternoon, the plainly marked trail left by the Amberley-Charbonneau party mounted to low hills stippled by piñon and cedar. The heat pressed like a great blistered hand from a lemon-colored sky; the sun poured savagely against their right sides.

Will Angsman rocked easily to his paint's gait, his relaxed alertness a part of his thought and being. He breathed deeply of the hot air, already savoring the sense of release that came when he left the habitations of men. Unthinkingly his senses catalogued the smell of cedar, a chicken hawk dipping against the sky, the hooffalls of their mounts and pack mule, the quickpanted pushups of a lizard colorless against a rock.

Such notice was second nature to Angsman; he'd lived for a time with Apache friends, but mostly by himself. He'd devoured everything the Indians could teach him, then had struck out on his own, which was why he could beat the Apache at his own game. Even Indians moved in an interdependent society. Necessity of lone survival had left Angsman with the knowledge and senses and sure serenity of an animal uncomplicated by thought. Lately, though, he'd had the troubled conviction that for a man, life could never reduce itself to such simple terms. . . .

Mexican Tom, pacing his short-coupled zebra dun alongside, mopped his sleeve across his brow. "Hey, amigo, we makin' pretty sorry time.

You expect to come up on them *cabrons* next year?"

"The sign says we're matching their pace. They're not pushing fast in this heat, neither are we. Not much over two hours ahead, and we'll make up the difference after nightfall, when they strike camp."

"We take 'em then, eh?"

Angsman nodded.

"Figure they be a fight, amigo?"

"Try to surprise 'em. Never can tell, though."

"That's good by me."

Angsman returned the other's grin, feeling a stir of affection for this thoughtless, mañana-living youth, so like him in some ways, utterly different in others. Together they had guided for the troops more than once, working in easy coordination with a paucity of words, their mutual understanding as two men of action being complete.

Aside from this Tomas Ramirez was his good friend; he'd plumbed past his outward inanities to a bedrock nature of unswerving loyalty and steady strength under stress, marred only by his one great weakness. He didn't get stupidly, ugly drunk, as did Jack Kincaid; he simply became boisterous, then befuddled, and finally passed out. His wasn't a raw or constant craving for liquor, yet it temporarily bridged some fundamental flaw in his nature, and to that degree filled a genuine need for him.

Angsman uncapped his water and took a small

swallow, afterward passing the canteen to Tom. Ramirez lifted it in wry salute, drank. . . .

Toward evening, as the last stratified rose-gold of sunset died along the western hills, they halted for a brief rest and made a cold meal off the last of the beef sandwiches Lupe had packed. Again in the saddle as twilight thickened, they pushed steadily on, guided by the first gleam of stars. Angsman could not track by dark, but he'd seen the Amberley's map and knew their direction of route; he also knew that the desert flats and rolling, sparsely wooded character of the land clear to the Toscos foothills would enable the party to follow it up without detour. Now with the cool of night setting in, he held a rapid pace, alert for the first sign of a night bivouac.

Along the brief eddy of an air current he picked up a faint trace of woodsmoke, mentioned this to Mexican Tom who shook his head. "Ain't arguin' with that Injun nose of yours, amigo. How far?"

"About an hour's ride."

Ramirez spotted the smoke wisping almost invisibly against the cobalt sky as quickly as Angsman. He answered Ramirez' half-seen questioning jerk of head with a sharp nod. Without words both men dismounted and ground-hitched their animals, working swiftly and silently.

They would separate here, Angsman whispered; he'd circle wide to come up on the camp from the south while Ramirez stalked the northern side. Each would work as near as possible, size up the layout from his own vantage, and pick his position. The signal to move in would be the hoot of a horned owl, and its reply.

The Mexican's assent was a mere nod; he settled onto his rump to slip off his boots while Angsman moved away on moccasined feet. He described a broad half-circle of the unseen camp, moving always nearer in a concentric line, till he made out the gently dipping bowl between a pocket of hills, filled with a ragged lift of scrub oak. The camp was concealed somewhere toward to the center of that grove, dense enough to hide their fire. Angsman could see only that fine banner darkly curling against the blue-black sky; next his ears selected faint camp-sounds from the other voices of night.

He went down the south slope of the bowl like a shadow, gliding noiselessly through the thorny brush encircling the oak stand. Shortly after he'd penetrated the first growth, flickering orange light grew against the darkness. Next the fire itself appeared through the tree boles . . . Angsman caught a sudden lift of angry voices. He achieved the low rimming edge of oak brush and there dropped to a crouch behind its leafy screen for a clear view of the camp.

He identified Charbonneau and his men — Ambruster, Uvaldes, a tow-headed stocky youth he'd never seen, and Jack Kincaid; following his habit, the half-breed was already the center of a flare-up.

61

James Amberley stood to one side with an arm thrown around his sister, Charbonneau stood with a slack negligence, yet defensively, between them and Kincaid. A knife flashed suddenly in the breed's hand, and Charbonneau moved like a striking snake. His fist made a meaty thud against Kincaid's bull neck, and the breed hit the ground on his hip and shoulder but rolled almost at once to his feet.

Charbonneau's three men were sprawled on the ground, indifferently watching while the leader and Jack Kincaid faced each other tensely. From the far side of the clearing drifted the deep hoot of a great horned owl. Nobody paid any heed, except for the dark, scar-faced Ramon Uvaldes. A cigarillo drooped from his thin lips, his eyes squinted against the smoke, and now his head lifted at the sound, twisting sharply at Angsman's low answering hoot.

Angsman was on his feet and moving forward as he replied to Mexican Tom's signal, moving quickly, because Uvaldes, sensing something amiss, had stabbed his cigarillo into the ground as he came swiftly up off his haunches, firelight glinting on his drawn pistol.

CHAPTER FIVE

The last rose-hued effect of the whisky had finally worn off, and James Amberley was fully and miserably aware of why he'd been so easily gulled into playing rabbit to Charbonneau's smoothly baited snare. The Creole had infused fresh life into his blasted hope of finding Douglas — an attempt that he felt must be made for Judith's sake, whatever the cost.

Not that Charbonneau wasn't possessed of a lethal charm to bolster his own self-argument . . . Amberley had the map and provisions for the trip and Charbonneau had a competent force of followers; why not join company? The good doctor had substantial funds; Armand and his men were presently at loose ends and could use this handsome payment for their services . . . in the event that they failed to find the gold, which, of course, all would share equally. A pleasant arrangement of business between gentlemen, *n'est-ce pas?* Of a certainty the good doctor, being a man of taste and discernment, did not believe the exaggerated nonsense of Armand's inherent duplicity that he guessed M'sieu the major had poured into his ears. It was true that the exigencies of frontier life did not breed archangels; but as to his personal honor, let no man cast slight on that of Armand Charbonneau, and was not a business arrangement an affair of honor?

Knowing few men outside of his own class, where honor was a thing taken for granted, Amberley was by nature trusting; moreover he had a myopic comic-opera view of the gentleman rogue. He'd muddily assured the Creole that he didn't doubt his integrity, but what of Bonito's Apaches, the necessity for a competent guide, and wouldn't Major Marsden object rather strenuously?

Charbonneau's deprecating gesture made nothing of these details. He spoke of his past fair dealings with the Apache, the nature of which he failed to mention; and Chief Bonito would welcome Armand as a *sheekasay,* a great brother. As to a guide, *voila* — was not the finest guide in the territory, Jack Kincaid, standing not a dozen paces away; would not this fine guide gladly accommodate his bon ami Armand? Also it would be most simple to circumvent M'sieu the major, a good officer, but sadly given to exaggeration. Armand and his men would leave the fort now and camp not far distant; in the early dawn the professor and the ma'mselle would rise and depart, well before the major had arisen, and ride to join Armand and his men. They would all proceed together to the succor of the doctor's brother; was not the scheme the essence of simplicity?

Simple enough, Amberley thought bitterly

now, and so was I. . . . In his drunken state, deceiving the major had held a certain savor of forbidden fruit. Even when they had joined Charbonneau well beyond the haven of Fort Stambaugh's walls, the Creole's attitude had not markedly changed. But as the whisky wore completely off, the man's winning ways began to ring falsely. At last the muttered exchanges between the others had completely enlightened the Easterner. . . .

Major Marsden's summing-up of this crew as cutthroats and blackguards had been only too accurate. Their talk was of nothing but the gold, and there was a fevered note to it. Whenever Amberley glanced at one of them, he met a silent and stony stare. These men would be of no help in their search, he knew then. They might even abandon them on reaching their destination or before — they needed only the map. Hard on the heels of that came a second cold realization: suppose they decided to kill them both in order to keep the secret of the gold, if any? Of course he'd heard that women could move in perfect safety among the worst of frontier desperadoes, but this was probably nonsense.

Judith too, though almost blind to everything but her purpose here, now realized their situation. She'd calmly shuttered any fear beneath the cold mask that armored all her emotions, sitting primly beside James now, feet tucked beneath her outspread skirt as she examined a broken fingernail. Where her wide-brimmed hat hadn't shielded her neck and lower face, she was badly sunburned; dust deeply discolored her gray habit and laid its powdered grit across her smooth chignon. She'd almost fallen after dismounting, and he could only guess at the punishment she'd endured in her soft condition and on that damned sidesaddle. But it wasn't these details which agitated Amberley's deepening worry; Judith seemed to be simply wilting away in this dead, suffocating heat. She'd hardly touched her supper. Her face glistened with sweat; it formed dark muddy patches on her clothing; she kept swallowing hard, as though fighting sickness, and her eyes, at first unnaturally bright, were becoming faintly glazed.

"Judith —"

"Yes, Jimmy?" Her response was falsely quick and bright.

"Are you all right, dear?"

"Quite." The smile cost an effort; her throat muscles fought convulsively at her tight high collar. Good Lord, Amberley thought in alarm, she's roasting to death in that rig — and corseted up like a dowager, I shouldn't wonder.

It spurred him to sudden decision. Another time he might have let her stew awhile in her iron hotbox and iron pride. Yet taken with their present situation, the fact left him suddenly shaking with anger. He had to get Judith out of this . . . and his mind came to taut focus on the revolver he'd packed in his gear. Better chance of getting his hands on that than his saddle

66

carbine. His gaze touched halfway across the clearing to his pack, and then he lounged casually to his feet.

"Sit down, my fran'."

Sitting tailor-fashion by the fire, Charbonneau spoke without troubling to glance up from the gun he was cleaning. Amberley felt his tight resolve harden, and with it a mounting wild stubbornness. He took a step toward his pack —

Suddenly glass broke on a rock.

Jack Kincaid had emptied a bottle he'd been steadily nursing for an hour, holding a black brooding silence. Flinging it away, he came to his feet, stumbling drunkenly, his mouth open and slack. His murky stare fixed on Judith as he started toward her mumbling, "Don't be skeered o' Jack, purty lady. . . ."

Throughout the day the half-breed's attention had hardly left her. Amberley had been half-dreading this, yet for a frozen moment he couldn't quite believe it was happening. Then wholly without thinking he lunged at Kincaid. The breed shot him a dully startled glance, growled deep in his throat and swung his thick arm as if swatting a fly. A hamlike palm clapped Amberley across the head and knocked him to the ground.

Dazedly he pushed up on his hands and knees. He straightened his askew spectacles, and the scene swam back to focus. Charbonneau was on his feet advancing toward Kincaid like a gaunt catamount. Amberley scrambled up as Judith rose uncertainly, putting his arm around her and drawing her back.

Charbonneau said patiently and without anger, "Let the Ma'mselle alone, Jack."

Kincaid hunched his great shoulders. "Naw. . . ." He squinted rheumily. "Break you in half, Armand. . . ."

The Creole glanced at the Amberleys, saying with a little shrug, almost apologetically, "No Western man do such thing, you comprehend. But Jack, he is not to blame. He is the pure animal —"

Kincaid growled again, suddenly stooping to tug at his boot. At once firelight flashed on a six-inch blade. Charbonneau moved swiftly, chopping a vicious blow to his neck. Kincaid went down, but came up almost at once. Amberley was obscurely aware that Uvaldes too had risen, his gun in hand. A voice that Amberley knew rapped out, "Drop it, Ramon!"

The scar-faced Mexican swung about; the pistol bucked in his hand as he shot twice at the bushes. An unseen gun blasted. Uvaldes, spun by an invisible blow, fell to his knees and toppled on his face across the fire. Glowing embers belched away from the smothering impact of his fall, and a dusting of sparks leaped and died.

There was still enough firelight to show young Staples and the giant Ambruster scrambling for their guns. Now a different voice said almost musically, "I wouldn', amigos."

Two men stepped from opposite flanks of the clearing, covering Charbonneau and his crew. Will Angsman moved in to place a moccasined foot against the sprawled Uvaldes' shoulder, roll him on his back. The body in its smoldering clothing was soft and limp and inert, and Amberley realized with a kind of distant shock that the man was dead.

The fire gathered back its steady outreaching glow, sallowing every face. Matter-of-factly, while his companion covered them, Angsman moved among the desperadoes, collecting their weapons. He pitched these into the bushes, afterward tramping over to Amberley.

"All right, professor? Your sister?"

"All . . . right," Amberley croaked. "My God —"

"Sit down, doctor, and take it easy," Angsman said gently. His shuttling glance lay hard against Charbonneau, and he tramped over to him. Incongruously in this shaken moment, Amberley noticed with surprise that Angsman was as tall as the gangleader; he'd thought of Charbonneau as loftier because the man theatrically dramatized his height, as he did everything.

Charbonneau grinned whitely, lightly resting his hands on hips. "*Bonjour,* old fran'. . . ."

"Always a new iron in the fire, eh, Armand? Long-looping, whisky-running . . . even a lost mine."

"Ah, yes, old fran'. But is legitimate business, no? Ask M'sieu le doctair. . . ."

"Get off the stage, Armand. There's your horses."

"I 'ave the agreement with M'sieu Amberley. I 'ave not decide to break it."

"Long walk might help you decide."

Charbonneau's smile thinned. "Do not do that to me, m'sieu."

Without turning his head, Angsman said softly, "Tomas . . . hooraw them off," stepping back then to cover the whole crew while the Mexican sheathed his gun and went to loose the picket line that held the horses. With Spanish epithets and lashing rope-end, he sent the gang's animals thundering from the clearing and through the brush, the sound of their going soon dying away. Grinning, he re-tied the Amberley animals.

"Leave your gear, except for a canteen of water apiece. Good twenty-five mile hike back to Fort Stambaugh — only if I was you, I'd try Contentionville. Marsden wasn't turning any cheeks, last I saw him." Angsman paused gently. "If you have got any further objections you care to state, go ahead. That's if you want to leave your canteens and your boots behind."

Charbonneau stood unmoving, still slack-poised, the fireglow washing wickedly against his eyes. At last he turned with the barest of shrugs, walked to the piled gear and got his canteen. The other three sullenly followed his example. Charbonneau, straightening with the strap of his canteen looped over a shoulder, let his glance briefly touch the dead Uvaldes, reserving his final

70

look for Angsman. Then he turned wordlessly and walked from the clearing, the crew filing off behind him. Angsman stood with his head tilted, listening to the crackle of brush with their passage.

After a full minute he let his gun off-cock and sheathed it, turning to the Mexican. "Want to get our horses, Tomas?"

"*Como no?* Then I bury that countryman."

"Have a care of yourself out there."

"Bah. That Charbonneau and his curly wolves not waitin' around; they blunder like the bull. Such *cabron* never surprise Tomas." The Mexican slipped easily away through the brush on his sock feet.

James Amberley mopped his brow with a bandanna. "Angsman, I can't tell you . . . you saved our lives!"

"Like enough," Angsman agreed drily. "If they decided to chuck you both off along the way, you'd last about a day. Got to hand it to you, professor. It took some reaching, but you made it — worse damnfool than you were yesterday. Get some sleep, the two of you — we'll be starting back at dawn. Don't argue that, Miss; I'm not in the mood."

Judith had been staring at the dead man, her face white and pinched; she started as though his words had shocked her from a trance. But her instant reply was flat and toneless: "I do not propose to argue, Mr. Angsman. Your help was welcome, but you are no longer needed here.

James and I will go on alone tomorrow."

"Reckon not, if you're tied to your saddle."

"If you touch me, sir, I shall scratch your eyes out."

A dead silence stretched out like a tenuous thread. . . . Amberley had the queer feeling that he'd ceased to exist in the mute antagonism that crackled between these two. It struck him that he'd never seen two people as many worlds apart, yet with so similar a blunt head-on manner. Quite suddenly he would have laughed aloud if the situation hadn't been so deadly serious. Judith's stare mirrored open contempt and defiance; Angsman's showed nothing at all.

Amberley had no inkling of his thought till the scout swung toward him unexpectedly: "Professor . . . you still want a guide, you got one from here out."

Amberley hadn't realized his own startled tension till he felt it wash out of him with his fast sigh of startled relief. "Gladly, sir — gladly." He added with a formal stiffening, minding Angsman's cold judgment of him, "Pleased that you changed your mind," and extended his hand. Ignoring it, Angsman swung away to stir the fire up.

CHAPTER SIX

"Stan' still, Angelito, you balky *chingado —*"

Mexican Tom fondly cursed the little gray mule as he diamond-hitched his and Angsman's gear to its back, and Angsman said without censure, "Easy on the mule-skinning lingo, Tomas."

Ramirez made a wry face, glancing at the Amberleys. "Sure, amigo, excuse it."

"By the way," Angsman murmured then, "you weren't committed to do more'n help me catch these greenhorns. Appreciate your joining up all the way. Can't have too many nursemaids."

"Por nada," Ramirez said cheerfully, adding with puzzled gravity, "Look, these . . . uh . . . Nuevo Inglés, they loco, eh?"

"That's it," Angsman agreed wearily. "Humor 'em, Tomas."

Mexican Tom covered his snicker by whistling *La Cacaracha,* and Angsman sent Judith Amberley a bleak glance. It hadn't been her blunt threat to fight him tooth and nail if he tried to force her return that had prompted his new decision. Irritably he'd told himself that letting her carry her search to its hopeless end was its own best means of punishing her blind, insensate arrogance; he couldn't let them go on alone when his presence might mean the difference between life and death. But this excuse had a hollow ring.

Somehow the antagonism between them had narrowed down to a personal challenge: at their first meeting when with acid candor she'd accused him of cowardice and again last night when she'd deliberately baited him with her contemptuous dislike. Without putting it into words, she had flung the gage of challenge at his manhood and dared him to pick it up. Angsman wondered with wrathful bafflement why he felt bound to prove anything to this headstrong and pampered woman, even committing his own life to whatever suicide pact she'd made with herself.

She was sitting beyond the dead fire, dabbing at her throat and face with a handkerchief she had soaked from her canteen, and now regarding her closely, Angsman forgot his anger — she was damned close to passing out. She appeared somewhat refreshed after a night's sleep, but the punishing heat of a new desert day was already taking its toll.

As he came up to her, she raised glazed eyes that held a residue of cold challenge; her prim chignon was undone, clinging in sweat-darkened strands to her cheeks, their feverish glow accenting her dead pallor. She was breathing quickly, partly through her mouth.

He said coldly, "That outfit belongs on a city bridle path. Likely to be your death here."

"I beg your pardon?"

James Amberley had finished tying his own pack on their animal, and now he came over with a frown of deep concern. "That's what I've been telling her. Jude, will you please listen? You can't continue another hour in that silly costume — convention be damned!"

"Nonsense, Jim." Her lips firmed thinly. "And I'll thank you not to swear."

Angsman said impatiently, "Got any spare duds like yours, professor?"

"Why yes, but I've put my pack together — oh, you mean —"

"Get 'em out. She can use one of the saddles Charbonneau left."

"How dare you!" The blood tiding against her sunburned throat showed a scarlet outrage even in her feverish weakness. "Are you — are you suggesting that I wear a *man's* —"

"You'll wear them, or we'll bury you before the day's out."

"Really, Angsman. . . ." Seeing that neither of them was paying attention, Amberley let his shocked objection trail. Again a clash of will, standing staring at each other.

Angsman, hesitating, decided there was no way to put it delicately. "Miss Amberley, you're shut up in a furnace of your own making, and an airless one to boot. You breathe mostly through your skin, and it cools you. Yours hasn't a chance in — in what you're wearing. Body makes its own heat and sheds it. You're not shedding, only taking in." He hesitated. "And you can't take the days ahead, the country ahead, on any sidesaddle."

She glared at him, biting her lower lip, and glanced at her brother as if in angry appeal. But Amberley was already unfastening their pack, letting it slide to the ground. In a moment he returned with clean, folded clothing; wordlessly he laid it at her side and walked away. Angsman lounged over to his paint, occupied himself fooling with the cinch. For a full minute Judith Amberley sat stiff and unmoving. Slowly and painfully then, she gathered up the clothes and climbed to her feet, disappearing into the oaks that fringed the clearing. Amberley relaxed with a sigh of profound relief, took out his tobacco pouch and loaded his pipe, moving over to the guide.

"Angsman —" he began briskly, pausing to strike a match and puff his pipe alight — "let's be frank. You don't like us much, and all things considered, I can't blame you —"

"Not that."

"All right, but why change your mind? I'm grateful, certainly — but why?"

"Man doesn't want his eyes scratched out."

Wry amusement touched the Easterner's mild face. "I realize that you Western fellows resent prying . . . but I wish you'd tell me one thing: is the expedition so utterly hopeless in terms of our survival? I'm steeled for the worst, but I'd like to know."

Angsman frowned his hesitation. "Lot to consider. I've lived and foraged alone in country overrun with hostiles months at a stretch. To give you an idea what that means, even Ramirez thinks I'm crazy for doing it. Here I'll have you three to look out for. Add to that that the eastern Toscos are as wild and rugged a stretch as you'll find in the territory, and you got a catamount by the tail."

Amberley thought a moment. "It must be a large area, though . . . and the Apaches surely can't be everywhere at once."

"They move around a lot. Their camps are built to be broke up and on the move in minutes. And their scouts, their hunting parties, cover a lot of territory. Just enough of us to be easily spotted — just few enough to make a tempting target. Another thing — you show Charbonneau your brother's map?"

"He studied my copy, but if he has one, it's in his memory." Amberley paused wryly. "I see your meaning. He can get fresh horses and provisions at Contentionville and take up our trail. . . ."

"And fast, with all that gold on his mind. By the way . . . what's your slant on that, professor?"

"I'm not bloodless, Angsman," James Amberley said dryly. "I daresay my dry scholar's soul is somewhat taken by the thought of a large treasure waiting to be picked up — as is yours."

Angsman grinned faintly. "How about your brother?"

Amberley bit hard on his pipestem, spoke carefully around it. "Why . . . I'm not wholly certain of Douglas' reasons. We were similar in our tastes, and close enough in that way, but the twelve-year difference in our ages didn't invite confidences."

"Make a guess."

The suggestion plainly discomfited Amberley. "Rather difficult to explain. . . . You've doubtless taken the impression from what we've told you that my brother was a rash and foolhardy boy. Rather, he was studious, a bit sensitive — and something of a weakling." He puffed on his pipe, embarrassed. "You might say this undertaking was a thing he had to do — to vindicate himself."

Angsman had been digging for useful information, and now from Amberley's cryptic and evasive reply, he realized that he'd touched cross-currents that went far deeper, probably involving all three Amberleys.

The Easterner added awkwardly, "Don't think too harshly of my sister. I can state without prejudice that she has some splendid qualities, not the least of which is being eminently sensible, once she overcomes a narrow viewpoint. Yankee practicality, we call it."

Judith Amberley returned to the clearing, very straight and stiff and resolutely refusing to hide behind the bundle of clothing she held bunched at her side. The grimy habit was carefully wrapped, Angsman supposed, around a discarded under-armor of stiffened whalebone, suffocating basque, and numerous unmentionables. Though the oversize trousers and shirt and light jacket she now wore were comfortably loose and shapeless, she was plainly struggling to hide a deep mortification, as though she'd shed, with a set of iron conventions, some defensive coloration. Her face had regained color with her new well-being, and it was evident she'd rather cut out her tongue than admit it. She walked to the open pack of her belongings, hesitated, then firmly dropped the bundle to one side. "You needn't trouble packing these things, Jim."

With this triumphant confirmation of her good sense, Amberley was prompted to say with completely untactful cheerfulness, "You know, in some warm countries I've been, women, uh —" At her icy glance, he blushed, muttering, "Rather becoming, though —"

She gasped, her martyred resentment flaming openly. "Oh? To be dressed like some painted saloon creature, or a — a circus performer? At least spare me that!"

Amberley sighed resignedly. . . .

Through that day they continued across rolling and semi-forested country, then struck on over a vast, level *playa* whose white-hot dazzling brilliance stretched away to the first foothills of the blued saw-toothed sierra; this shimmered to distortion in the heavy heat waves. Impalpable dust rose as they plodded into its waterless desolation, and the sun broiled against their faces and backs all that day, and several more following. Restlessly scanning their back trail through his Army field glasses, Angsman saw the riders coming as distant dots on the playa late in the third day. He said nothing to the others.

Charbonneau had lost no time. . . .

Moving onto the foothills, they fought through a jungle of mesquite, Spanish dagger, and cloudy white forests of yucca, until these gave welcome way to gentler open slopes of scattered manzanita and juniper.

On the seventh day, Angsman called an early halt, and while Tomas Ramirez and Judith Amberley gathered greasewood brush for a fire, he and Amberley pored over the *derrotero* spread out on a flat rock between them. Angsman traced a calloused finger along a wavering line that bisected the chart, which was now frayed and grimy and discolored by a brown waterstain. "Obregon's landmarks have placed out right as rain so far . . . and that should be the Paisano River. Far as I've ever been. From there on, this better be damn' well right."

"Hasn't the old Don's accuracy so far proven anything to you, Angsman?"

"Don't make the rest of it gospel. The man admitted he was out of his mind on the return trip."

Amberley shook his head. "You're quite an agnostic."

"What's that?"

"Word recently coined by a British scientist named Huxley. Means one who suspends belief until all the evidence is in."

"We'll see," was all Angsman said.

He glanced at Judith Amberley who was occupied in building a fire as he had shown her, arranging sticks to make a small concentrated blaze. He had to admit she was bearing up far better than he'd expected, performing homely camp chores without complaint. She had begun to harden past the first raw experience of aching muscles, blisters, and sunburn; after struggling for a time with the dusty matted tangle of her long hair, she'd cropped it off close to her head. The skin of her nose and cheeks was peeling. With her man's clothing, it made her seem slight and boyish and urchin-like, and the outward change had thawed a little of her chilly reserve. She had unbent from time to time to ask questions about the desert and its fierce teeming life.

Yet the upshot of it was that Angsman understood her less than before. She was a strange woman, at once woodenly reserved and candidly forthright, never revealing more than a little of herself at a time. He'd wondered whether the core of her was empty or sound; her incredible adaptability had answered him. Judith Amberley contained untapped reserve adequate to meet the demands exerted by even her iron will. It deepened the puzzle; she seemed to be all driving tensions, without a trace of womanly softness, and he could wonder now whether there might be depths to her no man had touched.

The thought was disturbing. Lately, some restless dissatisfaction which he recognized as a threat to his cherished independence had nagged at him, and he warily wondered whether Judith Amberley had somehow become tied up in his struggle with himself.

Suddenly his mind was emptied of everything but his alert senses. A strengthening downcurrent breeze bore the faintest trace of burning curl-leaf . . . hardly any smoke. That was Indian; and without a word he walked to the pyre of creosote twigs, scattered it with a sweep of his foot. Before she could form an angry response, he said curtly, "No fire. We've got company."

Amberley glanced up from his chart. "What?"

"Stay here, and stay quiet. Tomas, we'll have a look."

Amberley came to his feet in alarm. "You aren't leaving — !"

"No danger yet. Don't know of us, or they wouldn't be thinking about supper."

"Not Apaches?"

"I'll let you know," Angsman said sardonically, already rummaging into his saddlebag for his field glasses. He looped them around his neck by the thong, glancing at Mexican Tom waiting with his old Springfield slung under his arm. The two men scaled the shallow ridge above their bivouac and followed its wide summit south, holding to the slope below skyline. At the southern extremity of the ridge a large bluff rose like a flinty fist, this sheering steeply off above a brush-filled valley.

Angsman flattened himself atop the crumbling scale of the bluff, easing along on his elbows till he could get an all-over view of the valley. Sunset crowned its western end with pink and gold, and he analyzed light conditions for chance of sunflash, afterward training his glasses on the telltale smudge of smoke and moving down to its source. Though dense brush almost concealed the camp, he could make it out enough to be certain. Bellying up to his side, Mexican Tom grunted, and Angsman handed him the glasses. After a moment Ramirez murmured: "How you make it, amigo?"

" 'Pache. Small party. Came from the south, or they'd have crossed our trail."

"*Por que?*"

"*Quien sabe?* Renegades up from Sonora maybe, on their way to join Bonito. Only way to be sure is wait till morning, see how they head out."

Back at camp Angsman told the Amberleys what he had seen, adding that from now on the three men would divide a night watch between them. Shortly they would reach the Paisano River and definitely hostile country. This night Mexican Tom and Amberley would split the watch while Angsman caught a few hours' sleep, then returned to keep lookout on the Apache camp.

Soon after midnight Amberley ended his nervous vigil and woke both Ramirez and Angsman; while the Mexican took up his post, Angsman moved off through the night toward the bluff without haste. The Apaches, believing that the

83

spirits of their dead roamed the darkness and must do so undisturbed, wouldn't break camp till first light.

At full dawn he watched them move out through the brush toward the eastern valley, cutting straight for the heart of the Toscos. So they were heading for a rendezvous with Bonito . . . well, it didn't greatly worsen their position, at least for now. This band was holding roughly parallel to their route, but well to the south, probably along an old Apache trail.

As they crossed an open break in the dense mesquite and chaparral, Angsman trained his glasses in turn on each rider. He counted five fiercely alert warriors, all heavily armed . . . probably fresh from the latest skirmish in the hereditary war between Mexico and Apacheria. Traces of faded warpaint showed on dark faces. Now Angsman held on the sixth rider, feeling a thin backwash of surprise. This was a woman, small and slight of stature in a dirty and tattered cotton dress. He had the fleeting impression that she was Indian but not Apache — perhaps a captive — and then she passed from sight.

Angsman caught the last rider in his sights now, and seeing the heavy barrel-chested figure naked save for warband, a muslin loin cloth and hip-length moccasins of white deerskin, seeing the broad ochre-smeared face, he knew cold recognition. . . .

Chingo.

Angsman lowered his glasses as the file of

riders vanished through a steep cut in a ridge. His breathing was slow and even, but he felt the heavy thud of his heart against the bare rock. Till now he had augured a slim chance for their survival in Bonito's country . . . for the wily old Chiricahua would not fight except on his own terms, and if possible, Angsman had meant to give him no good chance. But that chance had just been narrowed by a deadlier concern than either Charbonneau or Bonito. . . .

The Amberleys were still asleep when he dropped back into camp. Ramirez gave his grim face one searching glance and said softly, "What is it, amigo?"

"Chingo," Angsman murmured. "On his way to Bonito all right. When and if he learns that I'm with this party —"

Mexican Tom whistled. "Man, this is not good."

"Not a word to the Amberleys. No need getting up more worry. If we're lucky —"

"Amigo, I'm scared that keepin' Chingo from smelling out anyone he hates much as you is gonna take more luck'n any of us got."

CHAPTER SEVEN

That night they reached the muddy wide millrace of the Paisano River where it cut down a shallow dip worn through lava. Here they crossed easily, pitching camp on its far bank. While the bitter light held, Angsman carefully consulted the Obregon chart, and afterward left the camp and ascended a lava ridge fifty yards away.

From this height he had his first view of the country east of the Paisano . . . a broken and desolate infinitude of mesa and canyon and naked rock. He was searching for a key landmark, and with a flicker of excitement he found it . . . a freak white streak that zigzagged like petrified lightning down the blue-black basaltic wall of a towering mesa to the northeast. The old Spaniard's chronicle had stressed that unusual formation; if he was further correct, beneath it would begin the huge pass that would lead through the Toscos to their goal.

Back in camp he told of his find in a few words, seeing Judith Amberley react to the news as a parched man would to water.

The next two days were pure hell, fighting their way across a treacherous upheaval of broken lava, slashed by tortuous canyons and ridges, toward the white-streaked mesa that had seemed amazingly near. The region was like a great raw cinder consumed by the burning eye of the sun arcing its fiery glance above. Nothing flourished here but the tough cholla and the spiked wands of ocotillo . . . no moving life except snakes or lizards which basked trailside in the sun and slithered from sight. They made painfully slow progress, covering most of the terrain on foot, fighting their skittish animals every yard of the way. Angsman called frequent halts while he went ahead to scout the best route along rimrock or canyon floor.

On the night they camped at last beneath the looming south wall of the mesa, everyone rolled exhaustedly into their blankets without food or talk, except for Angsman. Inured to the bitterest hardship, he held a watch most of the night, cutting Tom's and Amberley's to an hour apiece. Standing vigil on a basaltic height of land, he could see into the vast black gulf of the pass not two miles to the north, its high rims awash with moonlight, marking the last leg of their journey . . . *Obregon Pass*, he thought, for the old Don deserved that much testimonial.

By late dawn they were picking a cautious way down a rugged slide into the great gorge. Angsman didn't have to warn the others to go easy. A furnace-blast of heat reflected by the sheer high walls beat fiercely against animals and riders, holding them to a snail's pace. It was anything but easy going, for the flat canyon floor, nowhere less than a hundred feet in width, was strewn with massive jagged boulders and smaller rubble fallen from the crumbling rim two hundred feet above. Again and again they had to climb laboriously over a huge slanting slide where an entire section of rimrock had collapsed. Occasionally the walls were bisected by huge cross-hatching canyons which had flooded the pass with shallow ridges of alluvial sediment.

By now Angsman's main concern wasn't the Apaches nor the brutal heat that was wearing down each one of them . . . their water was running dangerously low. Ramirez had packed a water keg on the mule Angelito, shielded from the sun by other gear — this in addition to an extra canteen apiece. But they had found only one muddy spring since leaving the Paisano, and their remaining water was swiftly eked to a limit by the canyon's raw heat and glare relentlessly drying the tissues of their bodies.

At dawn of their third day in Obregon Pass, James Amberley carefully checked Don Pedro's directions against the distance that Angsman had computed they'd covered. "It seems fairly certain that we're very close to Muro del Sangre. . . ."

"Whatever that is," Angsman observed sardonically.

"In any case the pass should end there . . . can't miss that." Amberley scanned the map once more, gave a weary shake of head, and pocketed it. He looked a far cry from the casually immaculate Easterner he'd been. His ragged blond beard was bleached lighter than his sun-blackened face, and his corduroys were shapeless with sweat and wear, colorless with dust. Judith in her brother's spare clothes looked as disreputable. She was thinned to gauntness, her lips cracked and blistered, and the fine slim planes of her face now seemed bony and angular. Her movements were mechanical with the dullness of exhaustion. Angsman uncapped the last canteen of rancid liquid and passed it around, only pretending to drink as it came back to him . . . and in saddle again, they plodded on.

Less than an hour later Angsman felt a faint tension in his mount, seeing the animal's ears prick up. "We're near on to water, I reckon."

"But where is it?" came Judith's husky query, to which Mexican Tom answered, "Senorita — if Willie say water, it is there."

"Not me. Paint here. He's never lied yet."

Soon the other animals caught the smell, quickened their drooping pace. Ahead the canyon took a majestic, sweeping curve, and they almost stumbled onto the stream. It cut transversely down from the upper pass, fanning out here in a broad shallow flow, then vanishing into a side canyon. It was the purest of water, cold and sparkling and crystal clear.

Angsman studied the surrounding cliffs while he held the mules and horses, letting them drink a little at a time, this while his companions stretched out on the low bank, drinking and bathing their faces and drinking again.

"Come on, amigo! The water, she's fine,"

Mexican Tom whooped at Angsman. He whooped again as, hunkered down, he scooped his sombrero full and poured it over his head. Water darkly stippled his dusty clothing, glistened on his brown laughing face and matted his shining black hair to his head. Then his expression changed queerly, fixing intently on something between his feet. His cupped hands darted down and brought up a double handful of the streambed.

"Madre de Dios," he whispered. His mouth hung foolishly open as the water streamed off his head. "Patron de oro — *gold!*"

Amberley, bellied down, squinted at the pebbly bottom of the stream. "Good heavens," he murmured. "There's a fortune right under our noses —"

"Catgold," Angsman suggested. "Pyrites —"

"Ain't no catgold, amigo; ain't no flash-in-the-pan strike, either! Por Dios, take a look for yourself!"

"While you hold the horses," Angsman said calmly.

Swearing under his breath, Mexican Tom reluctantly left the stream to tend the animals. Angsman threw off his pack and dug out his prospector's gear. He stooped beside the water, aware of their fascinated concentration as he panned up a little sand and gravel bearing a flicker of sunny color, stirred it in an expert curving and rocking motion. He coaxed up sun-caught flecks of heavy metal, thinking incredulously, There's twenty dollars worth of yellow in this pan. . . .

He showed none of the keen excitement that bit into his usual cool perspective. It was no time for anyone to become infected with gold fever. "Middling good strike."

"Middling — ! Gold washes down, not up, *compadre*. This stuff, she's just float. Up higher they must be solid veins an' outcrops. We all rich, Santa Maria!"

Angsman said softly, "May be time later to think about gold. Want to go kiting after it now, amigo?"

Mexican Tom met his hard stare a long moment, sullenly let his own gaze fall. "Ain't no need you should ask that, hombre. I stick."

"Gold — and Don Pedro's stream. We must be close to the old Spanish diggings," Amberley said excitedly.

Angsman scooped up a handful of the pan's contents and examined it. Gold washed any distance from its source became polished by abrasion of rocks and gravel . . . these flakes were rough. The presence of much broken quartz indicated a source lode rather than placer deposits, he guessed . . . and damned highgrade stuff.

"I'd say so," he answered Amberley, and came to his feet then, assessing the surrounding terrain in detail, for this had to be journey's end. Obregon Pass ran at a gradual upslant for another half-mile, its main trunk terminating at the scarp of an almost sheer, flat-topped mesa. Toward its end the high cliffs tapered low, and studying the gray rimrock, Angsman saw a suspicious detail. It moved and was gone.

"Don't look up. We're being watched."

"Apaches?" Amberley whispered. "Then they know about us —"

"Have for some time. No enemy of Bonito's ever surprised him. He'd keep his scouts flung out wide, handpicked to a man."

The scientist stared a helpless question.

"We pick a spot, and fast," Angsman said quietly. "My guess, if we stay in the open, we won't live out another day."

"More likely, another dawn," Amberley muttered.

"Mostly they don't fight at night — has to do with their religion." Angsman smiled faintly. "Only they got their agnostics too, professor, so you could be right. One thing, Bonito won't attack till he's sniffed us out thoroughly, made sure of winning. With good cover and a lot of luck, there's a chance."

"What you propose, sir, is that we run and hide, like frightened rabbits." Judith Amberley's still-parched throat gave a shrill shrewish edge to her words. "We did not come all this way to crawl into a hole and hide —"

He met her hot, bitter stare, understanding her exhausted tension. He said matter-of-factly, "We need time to plan. This is roughly the place, but we haven't a notion of where to start looking.

Got to figure out what that Muro del Sangre is — assuming Douglas and the guide got that far — then study how to scout it out. Large order, that, and we got to stay alive to fill it. Set up a base camp, work out from there."

Amberley smiled wryly. "We're in your hands — as usual."

"I'll have a look. Tomas, keep a sharp watch."

On foot, Angsman cut across to the broad branch canyon into which the stream poured. He moved into it, working downstream along the left bank which was a shelving ledge two yards wide between cliff and water.

Shortly he halted by a small ravine which penetrated back several yards till it widened into a large bowl, roughly oval in shape, and boxed in by sheer walls which sloped gently off toward the bottom. At one end the cliff formed a high bulge, like a protective overhang, above a deep cleft along its base. Angsman nodded his satisfaction — with one man mounting guard at the narrow mouth, an approaching enemy should be quickly spotted. The cliff overhang would shield them from the rim, with a scattering of giant boulders for additional cover. Except for a drawn-out siege, this cul-de-sac was ideal; they had plenty of food and there was abundant water nearby. To one side a large patch of grass flourished in the lava soil — enough to last their animals a while.

The lowering sun had already gilded the rim-rock to a muted gold, and Angsman wanted to

set up permanent camp before darkness. Returning, he told the others of his find, adding, "Tomorrow I'll scout to the end of Obregon Pass
. . . see what I can find."

"By the bye, Angsman," Amberley commented
gravely, "rather nice gesture of yours, naming
the pass after the old boy. Didn't suspect you
of that much sentiment."

Angsman regarded his serious face a long moment, unable to decide whether he'd been
treated to a specimen of greenhorn humor.

Amberley took the first guard shift by the ravine mouth, sitting on a low rock with his rifle
across his knees, keeping a drowsy attention on
the canyon beyond, from which drifted the mur-
murous glissando of the stream. Behind him
Judith and Angsman and Ramirez slept circling
the meager warmth of a small fire which created
a weird dance of light and shadow along the
rugged walls.

Amberley's nervously excited thoughts were
shaded by disappointment at Angsman's flat insistence on investigating the terrain alone. By
George, the man was as bull-headed as Judith
. . . insisting that the others needed a few days'
rest, bluntly stating that they'd only be in his
way. Angsman had yielded only once, in his
reluctant agreement to guide them, and since
that time there had been absolutely no arguing
with the man. Damn it, he, Jim Amberley, was
no amateur in the wilderness. His archaeologist's

soul was itching to be present if Angsman should uncover the old Spanish mine.

A backwash of guilt nudged his conscience, thinking of how Judith's single-minded concern was with finding their brother. Yet, knowing himself, he could only be honest. He'd traveled to the corners of the earth without ever, in a sense, leaving his ivory tower. Amberley liked people, found them fascinating at times, but always as objects of his analytical curiosity; he'd always shunned personal involvement.

Maybe that secret shame of his own lack of responsive warmth had let him timidly permit a younger sister to assume the dominating role in their little family circle after the deaths of their parents in a train wreck ten years ago. That had been a mistake, and so, perhaps, was his failure to argue her out of this hazardous and hopeless search. But he didn't think so —

Suddenly he came alert . . . a dislodged pebble had plopped into the stream.

Something was moving up the black canyon gulf, hugging the wall at a dozen yards' distance, picked out by the faint light of a crescent moon. It came on silently in a prowling crouch. Shocked from his bemused revery, Amberley could only stare. Without thinking now, he brought his rifle to his shoulder, firing hastily.

The shot cascaded a pulse of flinty echoes from the cliffs; the figure scurried away upcanyon toward the pass, quickly swallowed by the darkness. And now Amberley's blood ran cold at the sound that drifted back . . . a moaning wail which climbed to a raging, maniacal scream. Angsman and Ramirez had already scrambled out of their blankets with guns in hand; the sound froze them in listening attitudes . . . then it died away.

"Mother of God," Ramirez whispered, crossing himself.

Angsman stepped forward, clamping a rough hand on Amberley's arm. "What was it? You see it?"

"Apache, I think. I shot —"

"Too damn' fast," Angsman declared roughly. "That was no 'Pache."

"She was no 'Pache," Mexican Tom echoed in a shuddering whisper. "Ain't nothing alive make no sound like that. This is place of the dead, *los muerto.* . . ."

Amberley said hotly, "I tell you it was a man, Apache or not!"

"Not an animal," Angsman slowly agreed, frowning. "You might have waited a little, professor."

"Lost my head," Amberley confessed lamely. "Had my mind on other things. Startled the devil out of me."

Judith had moved to her brother's side, and he could feel her uncontrollable trembling. He shared her sudden fear . . . of a thing neither one of them had considered. "Jim," she breathed. "Was it — do you think — it could be —"

"No." Amberley shook his head, trying to convey certainty against his memory of that chilling scream, and he thought now fervently, *I pray God it wasn't.*

Angsman eased the rifle from his nerveless fingers, saying quietly, "I'll take over, professor. Rest of you try to get some sleep. Better stick here till daylight; no point batting around in the dark. If there's any sign, it'll be there come morning."

CHAPTER EIGHT

When dawn spread its roseate glow across the gray rimrock and lanced scarlet arrows of first sunlight across the paling sky, Angsman left off guard duty and woke Tomas Ramirez, telling him to keep a close lookout.

"Sure, amigo." With daylight, Ramirez had recovered his lazy poise; he dexterously struck a spark into his tinder-cord with flint and steel *eslabon,* blew it to glowing life in his cupped hands and ducked his head to light the corn-shuck cigarette he'd rolled. "Gonna follow up that crazy laugh?"

Angsman nodded.

Ramirez lunged a deep drag, exhaled it almost reluctantly, glancing at the sleeping Amberleys. "You think it's maybe their brother an' he eat some loco weed?"

"Tomas, I don't know. Hell of a thing."

"Yeah. Well, I nursemaid pretty good. Get along, amigo; give a yell, you need help."

Angsman left the box ravine and swung up the branch gorge. Where the pebbly bank of the stream gave way to patches of soft sand, he found the marks of splayed bare feet, and thought wryly, A real wild customer. Then, leaving the gorge where it debauched into Obregon Pass, he came to a dead halt. Angsman wasn't a man easily disconcerted, and now he was held utterly motionless.

The facing wall of the giant flat-summitted mesa that ended the pass was, as he'd noted, of common red sandstone, though unusually smooth and straight, as though the elements had vied to crack and erode its tough substance and had only succeeded in polishing it to what, at this distance, was a softened gloss. The first rays of dawn, streaking across the heights, so angled their red glow against the smooth sandstone that instead of being absorbed or diffused it was flung back brilliantly, almost hurtingly, against the watching eye. Along the crest it flamed like red-hot iron. But the really striking effect was in the way the livid glow moved slowly downward, transforming the dull crimson stone beneath. It sent ahead big globular feelers that were actually the mounting sunrise gradually highlighting the faint swells and irregularities, creating the fierce illusion of a great bleeding wound streaming bright rivulets down the mesa flank. . . .

This, Angsman knew, could only be Muro del Sangre . . . the Wall of Blood. He was seeing it as Pedro de Obregon the grandee had first viewed it more than two hundred years ago, in an awed scholarly reverence that he'd rendered in riddle, so as not to violate some sensitive, if morbid, chord set to quivering in his poetic soul. Angsman, not at all a poet, understood his sensations exactly.

The effect was transient, and even as he watched, the sharp glow faded and was soon gone, leaving only a mundane wall of red sandstone under a hot mounting sun. Somewhere beneath that wall should lie the old Spanish mine . . . and with it, if he was lucky, a clue to Douglas Amberley's fate.

Moving upcanyon toward the mesa, following the bank of the stream, Angsman found more bare footprints. Their prowler had come this way. Angsman kept a watchful surveillance on the cliffs, knowing he'd make a choice target for an Apache scout.

He wondered if there was a bare chance that Amberley might be right, that Bonito might not trouble them while their intentions remained obviously peaceable. The old chief had brought his people here to avoid trouble, not to seek it. Still there was no cut-and-dried pattern into which the motives of an Apache — or anybody else — would fall. A lot might depend on how near they were to Bonito's rancheria. For on reflection, Angsman thought that Bonito probably had a permanent camp somewhere in this mountain stronghold. To feed and water a band of upwards of fifty bucks, squaws and children, taken with all their animals, was obviously the ancient chief's main problem in selecting his retreat. And Apache or not, providing for such a band in this barren and near-waterless range would require a special place. He made a mental note to find and size up the camp for a better idea of what they might have to face — especially with Chingo in the vicinity. . . .

Angsman felt a vast wash of relief when at last he turned into a feeder canyon with high sheltering walls, just beneath the looming height of Muro del Sangre. The stream issued from this canyon, and the footprints, scuffed and re-crossed along its bank, indicated that the intruder had often come and gone this way.

Suddenly, turning a sharp angle in the canyon, Angsman came to a halt. He had found the old fort built by Don Pedro and his companions.

It was a narrow, low-built structure with thick walls constructed of flat stone slabs and longer flat slabs laid above these to form the roof which wasn't over four feet across . . . crude but damned substantial. Evidently it had been originally built into a long deep notch in the canyon wall, but numerous landslides from the high rim had partly filled that notch. They had crushed most of the stone roof and cascaded inward. Peering through a low entrance, he saw that the interior was choked by boulders and debris, leaving only a dark cubbyhole toward the front. The old mine was sealed off for good. . . .

Gun in hand, Angsman ducked inside. Sunlight pouring through the jagged wall interstices showed this to be the home . . . or lair . . . of their wild man. A circle of blackened stones held the ashes of a cookfire, and scattered about were the bones of small animals, broken for the marrow. Angsman sheathed his gun and settled on his haunches to study the dirt floor, fouled with excrement and other filth. A dull gleam of half-buried metal caught his eye. He unearthed it with a root of his boot, picked it up. A battered and useless canteen, with a gaping hole in its side.

Angsman carried it out to the light and knocked the dirt off to examine it carefully. Deep scratches in the intact side formed the plain initials *D. A.* Douglas Amberley . . . ?

The identity of their prowler might be narrowing down, he reflected cautiously . . . if you assumed that an accident had left young Amberley deranged, a cackling madman who kept alive by scavenging for rodents, who holed up in this filthy burrow like a wild beast. But there was also old Caleb Tree who'd guided the boy . . . and one of them must be dead.

The other was likely worse than dead.

Angsman went over the ground now with infinite care, but found no more signs on the stony ground. The tracks had led into this canyon, so he must have returned to this lair last night — where had he gone from here? No telling, for he probably roamed the area freely, unmolested by the Apaches who would recognize his madness and shun him. Somehow he had to be run to ground and taken alive. . . .

If he'd been frightened off by Angsman's approach, he could only have retreated up the feeder canyon to its source on the rim above . . .

or to its dead end. The latter possibility was worth following up.

As Angsman proceeded along the narrow ledge bordering the stream, the canyon narrowed, confining the water as it gushed down the mounting slant into a deep and roiling torrent; its echoes chattered together in a thin roar between the high walls. There were flecks of heavy color here which indicated that the gold in the lower stream had not been carried from the old mine diggings, but from still farther up — a second rich lode.

Now the canyon widened toward its end — a box canyon. Here was the source of their clear cold stream, swirling out from a broad placid pool, fed by an underground stream as he'd thought. The gold ore must have washed from the rim somewhere above this point. Angsman peered briefly into the pool, finding it dark and still and sullen, as though bottomless.

He retraced his steps to the old fort, there pausing to debate whether to wait for the prowler's return . . . decided against it. The wild man's absence at this early hour suggested that he'd resolved with mad cunning to avoid his lair for a time; there were other side canyons where he might hole up. Tracking him down would require time and patience. Just now Angsman felt a strong curiosity to test Pedro de Obregon's veracity further — so far the old Don hadn't missed a turn.

According to Obregon's account, after leaving the fort his gold-laden *conducta* had been attacked by Indians. The men and animals had retreated up a trail to an opening in a maze of caves. Since gold meant nothing to the Apaches, a fortune in gold bars must still be intact somewhere in those caves. As he recalled Don Pedro's description, the entrance lay just below the rim on the south wall of Obregon Pass, approximately two hundred *pasos*, or double steps, downcanyon from the base of Muro del Sangre.

Emerging from the feeder canyon, Angsman kept a wary watch on the cliffs while he mentally counted his steps, working back down the pass along its south wall. Having paced off the distance, he craned his neck back to scan the cliff. A broad shelf projected about thirty feet below the rim, and above it a glimpse of what might easily be mistaken for a dark shallow pit in the rock. That must be the cave . . . but there was no trail, only a sheer hundred foot drop to the canyon floor. Still, the wall was rotten with age and erosion, its base heaped with tons of rubble. A whole section of wall could have scaled off and collapsed at any time . . . and with it the trail.

Discovering that he was ravenously hungry, Angsman decided to join the Amberleys for breakfast. His finding of Doug's canteen in the wild man's lair was no pleasant detail, but they needed to be prepared for the worst. So far both of them had borne up well. Angsman had to smile, thinking of how Amberley's scientific enthusiasm would be fired by his news of finding the mine. Might have to hogtie the man to keep him in camp now. He'd be like a kid in prospect of a new toy. With his lifelong urge to see beyond the next hill, Angsman could understand that, and he thought with a wry grin, Likely neither of us ever finished growing up. Amberley lacked his own tough streak of independence, and his occasional absentmindedness was annoying, but he'd showed adaptability, solid courage, and a keen mind. Angsman felt a curious liking for the man.

Returning to the branch canyon, he was about to swing into it when he came to a halt, hearing now a faint and distant sound, a chink of iron on stone. It came from downpass to the west — and shod horses meant white men.

Angsman settled into immobility behind a shoulder of rock that partly blocked the gorge mouth and waited. His dusty clothing might have been part of the sun-blasted rock. A chuckwalla lizard wriggled from a fissure a yard away, sensed his presence and promptly shrank back, bloating its body to wedge itself immovably within the crack. A hawk wheeled concentrically against the sky, dipped and vanished beyond the rimrock. It was very hot. A ragged trickle of sweat glided down Angsman's ribs.

The four riders rounded the sweeping turn in the pass, coming at a thirsty run for the stream. They flung themselves from their saddles and bellied down to drink — all but Charbonneau.

He knelt holding his reins and drank from his cupped hands, then stood hipshot and alert, letting his horse drink while he scanned the surrounding rocks.

"Hold them horses, mes amis, or they founder themself."

"Armand," Big Turk Ambruster croaked, "this heah look like gold . . . and they's a lot of it." His shining black fist rose with a handful of stream gravel. "My Gawd — *gold!* We gwine be rich!"

Charbonneau was unmoving for a moment, watching the excited scramblings of his men. Then he too was on hands and knees, with clawed fingers gouging at the streambed.

Angsman rose now, cocking his Colt as he stepped out to sight. The crisp metallic sound froze Charbonneau and Kincaid and Ambruster, caught on their hands and knees in the water. Only the blond kid named Will-John Staples seemed to take no heed, pawing frantically at the gravel and laughing and crying at once.

". . . We gonna have it now for sure, Lucy, that big farm and all —"

"Shut up, boy," Turk Ambruster rumbled.

Will-John's jaw fell stupidly, seeing Angsman; he climbed to his feet, mud and gravel slipping from his fingers. The others came upright too, all four watching Angsman with a kind of wary calculation as though they and not he held the gun, wondering whether they could take it and kill him and keep the secret of this gold.

"While you're thinking about it, get your hands high."

Sullenly they obeyed except for Charbonneau; recovering jaunty arrogance he drew a cheroot from his vest pocket and lighted it without haste. Angsman tilted his gun an inch downward and shot into the mud, spattering the Creole's boots. "Hear that all right, Armand?"

"Armand's hearing is pairfec'," the Creole grinned cockily, but he raised his hands. "My memory's pretty good too, 'specially for old Spanish maps. She's a free country, hein? Nothing to say we don't stake the claim here."

"Nothing to say I don't drop the four of you now. Can't find a good offhand reason I shouldn't."

"Because you are one damn' fool, you will not. Come, my fran'; leave us alone, we leave you alone. By the way, you 'ave find the Spanish diggings, eh?"

Angsman said gently, "You're movin' on, Armand."

"Ah, oui?"

Angsman gave a backward nod, saying flatly, "We're camped in there. You're a sight too close for our comfort . . . see that big slide yonder? You can get up the cliffs that way. Advise you camp back a piece from the rim — I see one of you stick his head over it, he's dead."

Charbonneau slowly sank to his haunches, lowering one hand to get a handful of gravel. He studied it thoughtfully. "Plenty rough flakes.

Means this drift stuff has not wash' far. We follow this stream, and —"

"You're way off, Armand. I followed the stream. Got an underground source. This stuff fell from the rim and got washed down here. Up there's where you'll find the lode."

"But the old Obregon mine —"

"Buried up under tons of rock. You'll never open it."

Charbonneau straightened to his feet, motioned curtly to the others. They mounted, the Creole briefly wheeling his horse toward Angsman. His green eyes were opaque and flinty. "The bargain, she work two way, M'sieu — stay clear off from us! A man is dead for a long time."

"Just so you don't forget it."

Drawn by Angsman's shot, the Amberleys and Ramirez now hurried up. Charbonneau murmured ironically, "Ma'mselle," touched his cheroot to hatbrim and cantered away. At the long broken slide indicated by Angsman the four men dismounted and began its ascent, leading their animals.

"So they found their way here," Amberley mused worriedly. "Will they make trouble?"

"Not unlikely, without they find what they're looking for up there."

CHAPTER NINE

Angsman spent the remainder of that day prowling the canyons and sub-canyons that opened in a complex maze off the big pass. He'd picked up fresh trail of their wild man below the mine canyon, but it soon petered out on bare rock. Through that day he saw no sign of wild man or Apache. The cliffs seemed to brood in the sun-shimmering stillness, waiting out the human intrigues that disturbed their ancient peace, in the serene knowledge that they would endure unchanged long after these human invaders had gone to dust.

So Angsman thought, and smiled dourly at himself. It was the sort of profound fantasy that came to grip a man who had lived alone too long in vast barren silences that hadn't been intended for a lone man. He realized with the unsettling sadness that came when a man faced some great change in his life, that this might be his last foray into such places. He'd lived alone too much, that was the long and short of it. He'd lived with the Indians and had recognized the great good of their simple and natural lives.

But he wasn't an Indian in heart or thought, and it was high time he faced it squarely. He was a maverick civilized man whose thoughts were turning more and more back to the society he'd repudiated. A man needed certain things — a wife and children and home — and he felt a strange ache, seeing in memory the green Virginia farmstead of his boyhood.

The following morning, up again with first dawn, Angsman returned to the old mine diggings on the slim chance the wild man might have returned. He was patiently scouring over the stony floor of the feeder canyon, when the noise began, startling him to poised alertness — a low roar of rock grinding on rock. At first he thought of a landslide, but the sound kept up with a steady, measured rumble, drifting down from the heights to his straining ears.

With mounting puzzlement he listened, fixing the source of the noise. He left the feeder canyon then and moved down Obregon Pass toward the slide where Charbonneau's gang had ascended to the cliff. Achieving its rim, Angsman glanced downward at a faint halloo. He saw Ramirez and Amberley, also attracted by the rumbling, leaving their canyon on the run. Angrily he waved them off, grimly waiting till they'd turned reluctantly back.

Then he struck back due south from the rim, moving at the tireless Apache jogtrot. He crossed one bare, canyon-riddled ridge and then a second, afterward threading through a forest of gigantic rubble. The roar was deafening now. He moved warily up near a lip of crumbling granite, seeing below it a round pocket set between the twin prongs of a horseshoe-shaped ridge.

Now he saw with little surprise the meaning of that steady, far-reaching rumble. It was an *arrastra,* such as the early Spaniards had used for breaking down gold-bearing ore. In the center of the pocket was a shallow pit floored with flat rocks, an upright beam set in its center. From this extended low crossbeams to which were lashed heavy rocks; as the upright post revolved, the rocks were dragged circularly around the pit, crushing the ore.

Also projecting from the upright about four feet above the ground was a long pole, to which was applied the motive power, usually a mule or horse. But this arrastra, Angsman saw with a coldness touching his spine, was powered by a man.

An Indian boy was pushing at the pole, his wrists lashed to it, feet digging at the stony earth. He was naked to the waist in the broiling sun; blood streamed from a dozen cuts on his lean coppery back and soaked his cotton drawers. It took plenty of muscle to even budge the arrastra, and the young Indian was faltering now, the long sinews of back and shoulders shuddering with his effort. But he was given no chance to rest.

Jack Kincaid paced the relentless circle with him, cursing hoarsely between pulls on a bottle in one meaty fist. In the other hand he held a thorny mesquite branch, and whenever the Apache broke stride, the branch curled viciously around his bare torso.

Stretched prone on his belly on the super-heated rock, Angsman scanned the camp. It was a permanent site, for they had built brush lean-tos and heaped their gear beneath these. Four animals including the two pack mules were hobbled nearby, skittish and wild-eyed with the strange roar. A great raw excavation showed on the ridgeside where chunks of ore had been torn out.

Young Will-John Staples sat cross-legged on the ground by a lean-to, twanging on a Jew's-harp, keeping time to the turning arrastra. He was bareheaded, and his broad simple face was sweat-shining and distorted by a queer fixed smile. . . .

There was no sign of Armand Charbonneau or Turk Ambruster.

They must have located the lode almost at once, for constructing the arrastra would have taken at least a day. The labor that had gone into it meant a rich strike, for only heavy-larded ore would satisfy these greed-crazed men.

At least it must have driven Kincaid and Staples crazy; evidently they had somehow captured a careless young buck, and now meant to torture him to death. For a warrior, such an end, measured not by its torment but by the humiliation, was the worst possible death. Angsman felt little compassion for the Apache who would have shown his enemies none. The Apaches had their own code and followed it pretty scrupulously, more than could be said for most of those who adjudged them bestial savages. Only cruelty and tenderness had nothing to do with ethics as the Apaches conceived them. Among those of the desert, beast or man, a cruel dying was accepted as matter-of-factly as the cruelty of life; it changed a man in fierce and subtle ways in his dealings with those not of his own people.

Entirely another motive prompted Angsman's sudden decision to help the Apache youth. So far Bonito had not moved against either party of whites. When the Apaches learned what had happened to this boy, the wary truce would certainly be ended, thanks to these fools. Saving the youth might also save Angsman and his companions.

He could handle Kincaid and Staples easily enough . . . he had no idea how far away Charbonneau and Ambruster were, but he wasn't waiting.

Gently Angsman nosed the barrel of his rifle over the liprock. His weapon was a '73 Winchester repeater, capable of getting off fifteen shots in as many seconds. He settled his sights on Jack Kincaid's wide chest, then tilted them a little aside, and fired. Splinters flew from an arrastra crossbeam. Kincaid stopped in his tracks, his jaw falling slack. Angsman sent two more shots into the dust at his feet and Kincaid retreated, wildly backpedaling; he tripped and fell and then lunged on his hands and knees toward the shelter of a lean-to. Angsman aimed carefully and snapped one of the slender supporting poles, collapsing the brush roof. With a deep-throated bawl of rage, Kincaid floundered away. The guide turned his attention to Will-John Staples who had grabbed for his rifle, leaning against a nearby rock. A spray of bullet-gouged sand stung his reaching hand, and he snatched it back.

Laying his shots down with systematic coldness, Angsman drove the pair to their feet and toward the far slope, egging their uncertain confusion into a direction of flight. They deserted their camp then in a scrambling ascent of the rock-strewn slope. Angsman left his own position, catfooting along the circular ridge crest where it joined the twin prongs, holding to shelter of scattered rocks. He wasn't a dozen yards from Kincaid and Staples as the panting pair topped the ridge, now swinging frantic glances to place their enemy. And then Angsman fired from his fresh position.

" *'Paches! — they're all around us!*" Kincaid bawled. He tore off down the outer ridge at a blind angle, heading for the cover of a deep distant wash, and Staples loped at his heels.

Angsman bounded down the long slope to the camp. The Apache's body sagged limply against the pole. Angsman reached his side, drew his knife and slashed the lashings on the captive's wrists. The boy's legs gave way and he fell. Roughly the guide hauled him to his feet and half-flung him into a drunken run toward the slope. . . .

Angsman worked back a half-mile toward Obregon Pass, mercilessly prodding the Apache ahead of him, halting finally in a nook between two sheltering rock slabs. The Apache fell to the ground, and Angsman sank on his heels facing him.

"Habla espanol?"

The youth gave no sign that he understood. He was heaving great gasping breaths, and blood still trickled from the long raw weals seared across back and chest and belly. There was no fear, no expression in his thin dark face; only the black eyes smoldering their unquenchable hatred and contempt. Angsman was fully aware of his sick humiliation at being snatched alive from a disgrace worse than death.

Speaking haltingly then in the slush-tongued Apache language Angsman said: "I use the tongue of the People badly, as you see."

The buck's hating stare betrayed no surprise; his mouth briefly worked, spat gummy saliva at Angsman's feet. The guide's tone held quiet and even. "I have killed Apaches, but as a man against men. I have not dragged brave men to death in the dirt, as a dog dies. There are two bands of *pinda-likoye* in your country. This you know well. You know it was not my white-eyes who did this thing. When you see Bonito, tell him of that, and of who saved your life and then spared it."

Then, because he knew that the disgrace of being captured and used like a draft beast would follow this youth through all his days, he added quietly: "The *Shis-in-day* are a proud people, and the pride of a people is a good thing. But a man feeds on the pride of himself, not that of others. The scars of the body are nothing; it is only the scars within that eat out manhood."

Without more words Angsman left him feeling the Apache's burning stare hold to his back till he was cut off from sight over a ridge. Swiftly then Angsman mounted a jagged buttress and flattened against its contour, there to take up a patient watch. His hope that his rescue of the young Apache would keep the Chiricahua from their throats was admittedly a slim one. He intended to track the youth to Bonito's rancheria and assess the odds they must face. And there was Chingo to consider. If he and his Mimbrenos had been heading for this rancheria, and this seemed certain, they had long since arrived.

One thing about those odds. They were bad.

Presently the Apache emerged from the nook, freshened by a brief rest, and set off at a painful jogtrot toward the southeast. Angsman left cover and followed him, calling on all his trail craft to hold the Chiricahua's track unseen. They moved on deep into midday, far into steadily heightening country.

Toward early afternoon, Angsman, about to skirt a thicket of catclaw, pulled swiftly back. A sentry was moving up on a bluff to hail the youth below. They passed a few words, and the boy went on. Having reached the outer line of lookouts, Angsman holed up to wait for nightfall. He made a meager supper off jerked beef strips he carried in his pocket, chewing them to a fibrous pulp and washing it down with a few swallows from his canteen. It was the crudest of fare, and the sun beat with blistering violence into the boulder field where he'd laid up out of sight of a chance hunting party or lone scout; sweat soaked his shirt and pants and pooled in his moccasins, and out of habit he conserved his water.

Once he caught sight of eight mounted warriors cutting the dust down a dry wash, headed for Obregon Pass — to avenge their young tribesman, he supposed. Charbonneau and his gang were in for it, and perhaps his own party. But Charbonneau would come first, and the wily Creole wouldn't kill easily; he'd hold the Indians off at least till night, and then they'd pull back till dawn. It gave Angsman time to use.

After dark he left hiding and descended into a canyon where the moon's soft rays did not penetrate, following its twisting course two miles west, knowing this would place him well within the heart of the guard perimeter. With heightening caution he left the canyon where it debouched into a valley and scaled a gently sloping ridge. Distantly he saw campfires pinpointing the night, and now he set to working in at a wide circle, holding his route below the ridge lines. When the first faint sounds of the camp grew ahead, he proceeded with utmost care, halting motionless several times when a fitful breeze arose so that his scent wouldn't alarm their horses.

Achieving the last ridge, he waited a long time before moving up onto it, alert to the smallest sign of a nearby sentry. The moonlight bathed the vast valley below in silvery relief, showing grass and forest. Down there would be abundant water and small game — this was Bonito's last-ditch stronghold.

The encampment was set off below this ridge. Angsman studied it through his field glasses. This was a typical Apache camp, with a half dozen small fires tended by women. The sizable remuda was confined in a makeshift corral of brush and rope, situated to the near side of the cluster of jacales. Angsman counted these, and made a rough count also of the grown warriors he could see — thirty or more men of all ages. Another eight with the bunch he'd seen earlier. A few outpost guards. The women were about half as many as the bucks, and there weren't many children. A band of about seventy souls, all told. The camp appeared quite haphazard and disorganized, and Angsman knew how deceptive was this impression: it could be broken up and on the move in a matter of minutes.

Idly now he moved his glasses across it, lingering on details. He focused briefly on one thick-set warrior and moved away, then came back swiftly with belated recognition. The man had just moved into the firelight; it clearly etched his broken flat face. Chingo, squatting now by a single fire with his five bucks — and the woman. Chingo and his hostile handful were no doubt enjoying a vacation, flushed with successful raiding in Mexico, but he and his Mimbrenos held warily apart from the Chiricahuas; the Apache tribes freely united only on the warpath, their ordinary relations strained and uncertain at best.

Again Angsman curiously studied the lone woman of their group, on her knees adding wood to the fire. She was slender and young. He couldn't tell much else from here.

For fifteen minutes he mentally catalogued the camp, afterward pulling back off the ridge to begin his circuitous return trek. He traveled a good ten miles by full moonlight, then halted to catch a few hours of sleep. He guessed that by now his companions would be deeply concerned, both by his failure to return and by the rattle of gunfire when the Apaches went after Charbonneau. Anyway they were safely forted, and there was Ramirez to handle any emergency. By setting out again before midnight, he should reach base camp shortly after sunrise. . . .

He shook away a last faint, nagging worry for them, and slept.

CHAPTER TEN

James Amberley piled more greasewood on the fire, watching its leaping blaze wipe back the night shadows banking the rough high walls of the bowl. He and Judith sat cross-legged by it, and now he glanced sidelong at her shadowed profile. In those last days, he reflected, the habit of silence had grown on them both. It was the savage, lonely quality of this country. It touched wellsprings in you that were deep and primitive, something not quite smothered by effete civilization. But the effect was an unsettling and half-fearful one; you had to be an Indian or a man like Will Angsman to take nature on its own terms — straight, and without Ralph Waldo Emerson's philosophical chasers.

This was Angsman's element, but even so Amberley was worried. After Angsman had waved off Ramirez and him when they'd started to investigate the mysterious grinding roar, they'd had no hint of his whereabouts. Ramirez had solved the noise: it was made by an old-time arrastra, sometimes still used in Mexico. But then came the rifle shots that had ended it . . . Angsman's no doubt, but why had he shot, and why hadn't he returned? Following his order, they'd stayed where they were, waiting out a nerve-wracking day. Then at early twilight had come more shots, an erratic flurry of firing that seemed to tell of a pitched battle. Soon it was finished, and they could only guess at what had happened.

Of course none of this necessarily meant that Angsman had come to harm. He was not, after all, unreliable, but uncommunicative, with an intense self-reliance that made him unpredictable and difficult to understand. Yet this was so integral a part of the man that you couldn't condemn it. Quite likely none of them would be alive now but for Angsman. In his own element, he was a man you couldn't help but like and admire.

Still Amberley wished with increasing unease that Angsman would return, for a new and immediate problem had come up. Mexican Tom had started to drink.

Ramirez had furtively produced the square brown bottle from his pack for a long thirsty pull shortly before supper. Later, bright-eyed and boisterous, he hadn't troubled to conceal his tippling, even brashly offering Amberley a drink. The Easterner had controlled his anger because in Angsman's absence they were wholly dependent on young Ramirez, and nothing could be served by antagonizing him. Yet aside from a heightening gaiety to stress his usual cheerful manner, the liquor hadn't appeared to greatly faze Mexican Tom, and he'd stowed the half-empty bottle away in his gear before moving jauntily out to the ravine mouth to take up the night watch. . . .

Quietly now, Amberley said: "A penny for your thoughts, Jude."

She sighed. "Hardly worth a copper, Jim. Only that I'm beginning to wonder — at last — if any of this is worth it. It's this country, I suppose. It's so big and naked and cruel that you can't look on the face of it and afterward be dishonest with yourself."

Amberley almost started in surprise. Her words had been spoken casually, but they'd hinted at a self-yielding of which he'd never believed his iron-willed sister to be capable. "Why," he said carefully, "that's rather odd, old girl."

"Coming from me," she said a little sharply. "Why don't you say it emphatically? Do you have to always be so — so pliable?" She broke off and laid her hand on his, saying contritely, "I'm sorry, Jimmy."

He said quietly, almost stiffly, "I've done what I felt I must, Jude . . . like you."

"Oh, I know . . . it's just that in all this empty silence, a person is thrown back on his own thoughts. Lately I've thought longer and harder than I ever could in my snug Boston cocoon. I don't regret coming here — it was a thing I had to do —"

"I understood that from the first. It's why I gave you barely a token argument."

"I know. You see a good deal more than I've

ever credited you for. . . . What I *do* regret is dragging two others, Angsman and Ramirez, into our situation. I baited Angsman quite deliberately into helping us, you know. Then, I didn't care how he felt, so long as I got what I wanted. Now — whatever his opinion is of me — it probably falls short of the bitter truth."

Amberley was silent an embarrassed moment. Then he said hopefully, "We're all alive and well till now — that's something. I'm sure Angsman will come back soon. And don't forget that prowler I scared off two nights ago. Angsman says that he is probably a white man. If so — well, we all called you foolish for insisting on what seemed a hopeless quest. Now, maybe we're the fools."

"Oh, Jimmy," she whispered. "If that *was* Doug —"

"If it was Doug, we'll find him. And make him well. You and I together —"

Behind them a boot grated on gravel. Amberley broke off, looking back over his shoulder. He felt a quick cold panic and stifled it with an effort, then came slowly to his feet. Judith rose with him, her fingers closed tightly on his arm.

Charbonneau stood facing them spraddle-legged; in his wolf-lean face, something harried and fierce and implacable warned Amberley to make no sudden move. Behind the Creole came a shuffling of feet, and Jack Kincaid emerged into the firelight, his dark broad face wary and sullen, pushing the staggering Ramirez ahead of him. The hulking Ambruster brought up the rear, supporting Will-John Staples. The blond youth slumped against the giant Negro, his head bent on his chest and shirt soaked with blood.

Charbonneau stepped forward to lift Amberley's pistol from its holster, ramming it in his own belt. "Sit down, doctair."

"What do you —"

"Do w'at I say, mon ami." The tone was flat and wicked, and Amberley obeyed, drawing Judith down beside him. Kincaid gave the young Mexican a shove that sent him sprawling at their feet.

Ambruster effortlessly bore Will-John's sagging weight to the fire and stretched him out on the ground, propping up his head on one of the Amberleys' blanket rolls. Charbonneau knelt by the boy and opened his shirt, removing a dirty compress. Blood welled cleanly from a hole high in the pale skin of his left chest. The blond youth's eyes were closed and his breath a harsh rasping; convulsive shudders wracked him.

The gravel-voiced Ambruster rumbled with an odd gentleness, "How he doin'?"

Charbonneau cuffed his hat awry on his head, rocking back on his heels. "He ain't good. Me, I think he don' make it. The damn' young fool." He spat sideways, glaring up at Kincaid. "You too, Jack."

Ambruster growled, "Be plenty time later for fetchin' down blame, Armand. Best we look to helpin' this boy."

"Oui. Fetch some water from the stream."

Charbonneau expertly cleaned Will-John's wound while Ambruster rummaged through Amberley's duffle and found a fairly clean shirt which he tore into strips for bandages. Amberley settled a bitterly accusing stare on Tomas Ramirez, who refused to look up, sitting with his head hung between his knees.

Then the Easterner's attention was diverted by Jack Kincaid, sitting off to the side in black silence, his hot murky stare fixed on Judith. If he makes a move toward her, I'll kill him, Amberley thought with cold decision. I'll get my hands on a gun and kill him. Beyond that silent promise, he warily decided to offer no resistance. Charbonneau could have killed him and Ramirez at once, had that been his intention.

Ambruster supported Will-John half-upright as Charbonneau affixed the bandage tightly around his torso, then eased him back and covered him with a blanket. Charbonneau then began to untie a bloody rag wrapped around his own wrist.

"Did you kill Angsman?" Amberley blurted point-blank.

Charbonneau glanced up with a grunt. "Why you think so, eh?"

"I don't believe you'd dare come here otherwise."

Charbonneau laughed shortly. He washed his flesh wound with clean water, fumbled a dry bandanna from a coat pocket with his good hand, caught an end of it in his teeth, wrapped it tightly around his wrist as he muttered a brief explanation.

They had found gold in the heights above, he said, a whole ridge larded with highgrade ore, and had built an arrastra to crush it out. But before they set to work, Charbonneau decided to try locating the rancheria of Bonito, which from the Apache signs he'd found, must be nearby. He had once sold repeating rifles to the Chiricahua leader, and hoped that by this past relation he might somehow dicker the old savage into letting them work their claim unmolested. The fact that Bonito hadn't as yet made a hostile move had emboldened him to make the try.

Early this morning he and Turk Ambruster had set out to find the rancheria, working in a wide circle toward the south. Having no success, they had started back when they heard the distant roar of the arrastra. Charbonneau's first fury at Kincaid and Staples for disobeying his orders had changed to sudden concern when he heard the whipcrack of a rifle, then the abrupt halt of the device. Urging their jaded animals toward camp, they'd found Staples and Kincaid cowering in a wash. Sorting out their blurted explanations, Charbonneau had learned that in his absence a young Apache buck spying on their camp had rashly ventured too near; a chunk of crumbling scale had broken off and tumbled him down the slope practically into their arms.

Charbonneau came to his feet now, awkwardly knotting the bandanna. His voice was flat and angry: "It was prime chance to show the Apach' our good faith, eh? But do these stupid cochon think of that? Non! Jack, who get drunk soon as I leave, now hitch the Apach' to the arrastra and 'ave the big fun making of him the mule to grind the gold. The Will-John go along, being not too bright as you comprehend; also he is not right in the head since we find the gold. It is maybe fifteen minute 'ave pass, someone start shooting down into the camp and drive our stupid ones off. When we come back with them, the Apach' is gone. Someone 'ave cut him free."

Amberley said tensely, "The Apaches?"

Charbonneau had finished tying his bandage; it freed his good hand for an expressive angry gesture. "Non, the Apach' would 'ave kill' our stupid ones, n'est-ce pas? And where is Angsman?"

Amberley shrugged coldly. "Gone since early this morning."

Charbonneau spat his anger. "That is w'at I figure. M'sieu Angsman is brought to our camp by the arrastra. It is he who free the Apach'. He think that will help him and you."

Understanding now, Amberley said slowly, "The Apache brought his friends back — they attacked your camp. Those were the shots we heard a while back. . . ."

"Oui. But Armand think this may 'appen; already I 'ave move our camp a distance away. They find us, but at least we are holed in the rocks, we fight them off till dark. We kill no

127

Apach', but Will-John is hurt bad; me, I am only scratch'. I know it is up with us; man can't fight the dirty Apach' on his own ground. We must try to get away in the night when the Apach' not fight. . . ."

A faint grin curled his bearded lips. "We 'ave to sneak out on foot, leaving the horse and the gear. This is not good, so Armand get the idea — why not come to this place which mus' be the fine fortress, for 'ave not my clever fran' Angsman chosen it? Here will be water and food. Here too will be gold. Not so much as up above, but that is now lost, eh? Armand is ver' sad for this. If your so-fine guide 'ave not let that Apach' go alive to tell his friends, it would not 'appen."

Amberley cleared his dry throat, saying coldly, "You'll kill us then, I suppose."

The Creole took a twisted cheroot from the waning supply that had bulged his vest pocket, eyed it regretfully, then bent and picked up a burning twig from the fire. "I tal' you, my fran' " — he puffed the cheroot alight, squinting at Amberley through the smoke — "Armand is not the saint. But I like you, this was not the fake, nor am I the ravisher of fair ladies." He gave Judith a slight courtly bow. "It is ver' simple . . . be good an' you live a while. The Mex, too." Chuckling, he rooted Ramirez in the ribs with a boot. "We expect trouble coming in here. The Mex, he is pretty sorry guard; he is sleep' like the babe in arms. . . ."

He broke off, glancing irritably at Kincaid,

who was rummaging noisily through Ramirez' pack. With a grunt of satisfaction he came up with the half-empty bottle, yanked its cork with his teeth. "Figgered that greaser'd been drinkin' something fierce," he announced, tilting it to his lips.

With a savage oath Charbonneau dashed his cheroot to the ground and took three swift steps, snatching the bottle from Kincaid's hand. A flick of his arm and it sailed into the darkness, shattering on an unseen rock. "That 'as cause us grief enough!"

Kincaid pivoted in a half-crouch, hand darting to the bone-handled knife in its boot-sheath. The cocking of Charbonneau's pistol froze him in mid-motion, its muzzle less than a foot from his head.

"Lemme break his goddamn breed neck, Armand," the Negro rumbled. "Been nothin' but trouble, him. Missed more sign'n he's found. Gwine git us all killed yet. . . ."

The half-breed hissed, "You try it, Armbuster," but he was careful not to move.

"But no, Turk," Charbonneau said gently. "Jack is but the animal, the big dumb animal. The rutting swine can be tamed, eh? Jack will be a good boy now. Eh, Jack, w'at you say?"

Kincaid barely nodded.

"This is ver' good of you," Charbonneau purred. "Go out now and mount the guard. I think with no whisky you keep the sharp eye."

Kincaid muttered, "Ain't no 'Paches gonna foller us at night."

"Not the Apach', you stupid cochon. Angsman. He is out there someplace, he may return tonight. He will come like the shadow." Charbonneau grinned wolfishly. "Keep the ver' sharp eye, my fran', or he see you first. The slaughtered pig does not rut good."

Kincaid picked up his rifle, paused momentarily with a sweep of hating black eyes that touched them all in turn, lingering lastly on Judith Amberley. His eyes narrowed, squinting almost shut, and he licked his lips. Abruptly he swung away and vanished noiselessly down the ravine.

Charbonneau let his pistol off-cock and slapped it into his holster. "So. Now we all sleep sound, I think. . . ."

Amberley woke with the first gray seep of false dawn, struggling half-upright in his blankets by the dead fire. With some vagrant sense of unease, he rubbed his eyes and swung a sleep-drugged glance around the camp, then settled it swiftly to his sister's blankets. These were bunched in a wadded heap on the scuffed ground. She was gone.

"Judith!" It left his throat in an agonized croak as he came to his feet. He thought of Kincaid, and even as the thought formed he was charging down the rocky corridor to its mouth. Kincaid was not on guard. Amberley plunged into the canyon and up the shelving stream bank. He

stumbled twice, almost falling into the rushing current.

Where the canyon debouched into the broad span of Obregon Pass, he brought up in his tracks, straining his eyes against the dim half-dawn stillness. *"Judith!"* The stony echoes mocked his thin shout, and then he sank down against a rock, rubbing a shaking hand over his face.

No great trick for the half-breed to stalk soundlessly into camp while they slept, and how he had taken her away without a noisy scuffle did not matter. It was done. The man was an utter animal, without restraint or moral sense.

"I should have known — I should have known!" Amberley groaned aloud, smashing his clenched hand against a rock. The sharp pain shocked him to the need for practical action.

Hurrying back to camp, he found the others awake. Ramirez was staring at the ground with a deep sickness in his face. Ambruster was bending above Will-John Staples who was babbling deliriously to somebody named Lucy about the farm they would buy.

"Hush up, boy." Ambruster's harsh bass was curiously gentle, deep and soothing. "You gwine open you wound with all that thrashin' 'bout, then you really have somethin' . . ."

Charbonneau was on his feet, scowling and assessing the situation, swearing with a savage tonelessness as he lighted a cheroot.

"Got to help me," Amberley panted. "My sister — Kincaid —"

The Creole blew smoke, his scowl deepening. "I 'ave seen, M'sieu. Do not tal' me more. It is ver' bad thing. I would 'ave shoot Jack las' night if I know w'at is in his dumb-ox head. But now it is done. The poor little lady. But she is the lucky one, maybe. W'atever he do to her — my fran', it is nothing to w'at the Apach' do to Jack when they find him. . . ."

"My God, man — you mean you won't — ?"

"Do w'at, eh?" The Creole's voice softened then. "I am ver' sorry for this, professair. Now it is daylight, the Apach' will kill any of us they find. They are waiting out there. In here is cover, is food and grub. We stay here a long time and hold off the Apach' — in time maybe find the way out." His fierce frown fixed on the cheroot smoke wreathing up in the still dawn air, avoiding Amberley's unbelieving stare. "It is too late, or I would go. Now, is hopeless. We only get ourself' kill'."

James Amberley was a man of logical bent, and the relentless logic of the Creole's words wasn't to be argued. Without replying, he pointed to his pistol in Charbonneau's belt. The Creole silently handed it to him. Amberley holstered it and went to his gear. Dug out a pasteboard box of rifle cartridges and rammed it in his coat pocket. He picked up his rifle, found his hat and tugged it on, left them without a backward glance.

Emerging into Obregon Pass, he began the hopeless task of scanning for sign. In his sweating concentration, he barely glanced at Tomas Ramirez as the youth shuffled softly to his side, extending one of the two canteens he held. After a moment Amberley took it, slipping the strap over his shoulder. His cold eyes met Mexican Tom's dark ones, seeing the somber stunned sickness there.

"Better get back with them," Amberley told him coldly. "Safer there."

"It is my doing, no?" Mexican Tom said softly. "If I am not drunk and asleep when they come, this would not 'appen."

Amberly did not answer, his face held stiff and unrelenting. More softly then, Ramirez said, "I am the tracker, you are not."

Amberley released a deep sigh of assent, saying brusquely, "Let's not waste time."

"It may be the long trail. I think the horses would be good to have. It is for you to say."

Briefly Amberley studied the dark young face, feeling a faint shock now, seeing there all the resigned fatalism that Ramirez' conquered and downtrodden people had learned in three centuries. He was ready to die to expiate his mistake, and fully expected to do so.

Amberley gave a slow, weary nod. "Get the horses, Tomas."

CHAPTER ELEVEN

True dawn had streaked the sky when Angsman topped a rugged promontory on his last leg off the heights down to the complex of gorges toward the end of Obregon Pass. He halted to alertness, hearing the faint drift of shots from far below. Evidently Charbonneau's crew had retreated into these canyons to make their last-ditch stand. With the new day, the Apaches had taken up the fight once more, and Angsman considered their plight without pity. They had pushed their greedy gamble too far, and must pay a grim piper.

Then, moving across a craggy rim before the last drop into the canyons, he paused curiously. A line of riders, like a file of ants, showed briefly to view on the floor of a distant shallow wash, then were cut off once more. That would be the raiding party, evidently headed back toward the rancheria. He supposed that those shots had accounted for the last of the Creole and his men, and tonight there would be a celebration in the lodges of the *Be-don-ko-he*.

Still, a faint worry for his own companions was revived in Angsman's thoughts. Though he had no doubt of Ramirez' ability to deal with any emergency, it had now been twenty-four hours since he'd left the base camp. Anything might have happened in that time.

An hour later he was nearly to Obregon Pass, swinging out of a rocky defile into the broad wash where he'd seen the riders. From the sign, they had both come and gone this way. And then, moving on, he heard the first faint sounds of a man in agony, and steeled himself. He turned a sharp bend and found Jack Kincaid. They had taken him alive.

He was stripped naked and lashed upright against a giant *bisnaga,* facing it. His wrists were bound together by a length of green rawhide circling the barrel cactus, hugging his arms around its spiny hulk in a fatal embrace. Other rawhide strips anchored his chest and waist. These had shrunk rapidly in the oven-blast of the mounting sun. His legs were splayed out and quivering, feet digging great furrows in a last terrible effort to push away from the barb-tipped spines. They had pierced his body in a hundred places, face and trunk and limbs, and blood, dried and fresh, covered him from head to foot and made a dark mire around his feet.

Like all Apache methods, this one was as exquisitely lingering as it was certain. Yet the bubbling moans were ebbing away, and only the convulsive quiver of tortured flesh showed a residue of life. Angsman had cut the last rawhide strip and eased Kincaid slowly off the excruciating barbs and onto the ground when the clink of shod hoofs on stone alerted him to horsemen moving up the wash. He had the startled thought that at least two of Charbonneau's crew still lived, and now he picked up his rifle and faded back to the turn, blending motionlessly against the bank.

Then Amberley and Ramirez rode into view, halting their skittish horses. Amberley half-fell out of his saddle and walked over like a man in a trance to the bloody, naked form. Angsman stepped out then, and Amberley lifted his glazed stare, whispering, "My God."

Mexican Tom dismounted, his dark eyes strangely haunted, and then realizing that Judith wasn't with them and that Amberley appeared in a state of near-shock, Angsman rapped out, "What's happened?"

Ramirez told him, giving himself the weight of blame. Angsman, listening with his head bent as he studied the ground, didn't censure him by a word. The thing was done, and Ramirez' voice held a misery to which nothing could be added. He himself shared blame, Angsman knew, for failing to return to camp yesterday. It stood to reason that Ramirez would have a bottle he hadn't found stashed somewhere.

The sign was badly scuffed, but enough remained to show how Kincaid, dragging Judith with him, had been surprised and wounded by the waiting Apaches, who then, satisfied with the double coup of bloodily revenging their young tribesman and taking a white woman captive, had headed triumphantly back for the rancheria.

He briefly explained this, and as his words struck through Amberley's grieving stupor, the Easterner said, "She — she's alive then? But merciful God —"

"On a far raid, they're likely to rape and kill," Angsman said thoughtfully. "This close to their camp, they'll take her there. She'll be slave to the buck that took her. Mostly they don't fancy white women. But they're like us, exceptions to every rule."

Amberley stared at him, white-faced. "Are you out of your mind?"

"What I'm pointing out," Angsman said thinly, "is she's alive and well . . . for which you can thank the Apaches. The rest is up to us."

"I — I'm sorry, Angsman. I should have known. But is there a chance?"

"Man can only try, professor."

"Going to be hell finding that Chiricahua camp, amigo," Mexican Tom said soberly. "This, she's a hard place to track."

"I found it yesterday — that's why I didn't make it back. I saw the bunch that has Miss Amberley swing southeast an hour back, following this same wash."

"Did you see her?" Amberley asked eagerly.

"Spotted 'em from that big bluff over east." Angsman swung his arm in a spare gesture. "Too far to more'n barely make 'em out. I came back here as the crow flies, but I was on foot, covering damn' rough terrain. Too rough for horseback-ers. These 'Paches are mounted. So they're swinging wide, but along an easier trail. I got the lay of the land though, and we can follow 'em faster their way. See you brought the horses." He nodded toward his and Judith's mounts tied to Ramirez' dun by lead ropes.

"Yes — we hoped we'd run into you — and find her, of course." Amberley dragged his reluctant gaze down to the now-silent body of Kincaid. He shuddered. "What about — ?"

"We'll be back this way — I hope." Angsman moved to his paint and swung into saddle, his face grim and tight. That hope was damned slim. Even if he could get into the rancheria alive, there wasn't only Bonito to face out. There was Chingo, who wouldn't rest till either he or Will Angsman was dead. But there was no choice left now. . . .

It was high noon when they approached the first wave of barrier ridges that guarded Bonito's valley. Against Amberley's chafing impatience, Angsman had held them to a steady, unhurried pace. Their horses were well-rested, and had to be conserved against future need.

He had no clear-cut plan for effecting Judith Amberley's rescue, for only one thing was certain: there was no possibility of taking the girl alive from an Apache camp by stealth or force. Whatever hand was dealt him had to be played boldly and openly.

As the three men rode up from a last dusty wash into sight of the first ridge, Angsman raised his hand for a halt, surveying its bare summit.

As the others ranged up beside him, he said quietly, " 'Pache sentry up there who's seen us by now, or I'm a liar."

"Do you see him?" Amberley demanded.

"No. Just the first likely place on this horse trail." He paused to isolate his next words. "You'll be staying here, the both of you. I'm going on alone."

Against their strenuous objections, he made his patient, reasoned argument. It wasn't a question of courage or even of duty. Three armed men would draw lightning; a single man stood the best chance of bluffing himself alive into the camp. Angsman was the logical one, knowing the customs and the language.

Ramirez' silence was his reluctant agreement; Amberley gave a slow and painful nod, and then, as Angsman started to dismount, the Easterner reached out to grip his arm. "Angsman —" he swallowed hard — "whatever you have to do — don't fail her."

Angsman stepped to the ground, tossed his reins to Ramirez, and leaving his rifle in its boot, tramped the fifty yards to the base of the ridge. He halted there, feeling the first crawl of strong tension as he watched the sun-scorched ridgetop. Nothing moved in the heat-dancing stillness. He unbuckled his pistol belt and let it fall, drew his hunting knife from its sheath and discarded that. He raised his voice in the Apache tongue: "I come as friend today, as I came yesterday to one who was whipped by the pinda-likoye who's

139

now died for that thing."

His words trailed into the waiting silence, and Angsman let it run on for a half-minute before he spoke again, now with a taunting edge: "My weapons are on the ground. Does the Be-don-ko-he fear that one man, alone and unarmed, will rout the People like frightened rabbits?"

A lean dark form glided up to view, his rifle ready but only half-raised. The buck's tone was low and contemptuous. "If a great noise could frighten the People, they should fear you, white-eyes who fights with his mouth." He spat briefly. "What do you want here?"

"I'd speak to Bonito. Today a white-eyed woman was brought this way by your warriors. I would speak of her."

"How do you know of this?"

"The woman was stolen from my camp by the bad pinda-likoye. We found his body. Your warriors took the woman."

"You followed them quickly."

"I knew of your camp."

"You lie, white-eyes. Only the Apache knows of this place."

"I found it yesterday — and spied on it by darkness. Tell Bonito not to post boys for sentinels."

The Apache was momentarily silent; a hint of grim respect touched his voice: "The woman is yours?"

Angsman said "Yes," without hesitation, because the Apache would appreciate the simple and direct. The sentry's glance flicked above his head. "And the two others?"

"They'll wait my return." He gave the words just enough bold assurance.

Abruptly the Apache left the ridgetop, descending with an easy grace, and then he motioned Angsman to precede him. They entered a deep notch that cut through this ridge and two more. The last ridge tapered off, ending the notch, and the rocky ground dissolved into a grassy gentle slope as they descended to the valley.

Approaching the rancheria, its sights and sounds and smells washed through Angsman's senses with the not-unpleasant memory of other camps . . . the smoke of greasewood fires, the smell of roasting muleflesh, the nopal drying, the grazing remuda tended by adolescent boys, the children running and playing among the pyramidal brush wickiups. A curious throng began to follow apace as Angsman and his guard moved toward a centrally placed jacal.

He did not see Judith Amberley . . . nor Chingo. Angsman held his face tight and his muscles loose, swinging easily ahead of his guard. He had only his patience and nerve and wit and his knowledge of these people; if they weren't enough, he would die a worse death than Jack Kincaid, for there would be warriors here who knew him. He could run no bluff; his speech must be as true as it was careful.

Two men stood by the jacal, quietly talking;

141

both ignored the approaching hubbub until Angsman's guard spoke to one of them. Though he'd never seen the Apache leader, Angsman knew that he was facing Bonito.

Almost diminutive in stature and further bent and withered by age, he was far from impressive at first glance. An ordinary warband confined his straight gray hair, and he wore a faded calico shirt and hip-length moccasins. His only adornment was a shiny, worn object hanging from his thin, sinewed neck by a rawhide cord — it was, Angsman realized wonderingly, a saint's medallion. Because Bonito was nothing if not all Apache, this one ironically displayed token — or trophy — bore strongly home to the white scout that within this shabby ancient little man lay an enigmatic depth of character that only a fool would take lightly.

He glanced briefly at Bonito's companion, the same youth he had rescued from Charbonneau's camp yesterday. The smooth young face was stony, his eyes unblinking as they met Angsman's.

Bonito listened to the sentry's words, his face a shriveled and unchanging mask. But his eyes were alert black lightning, flickering from Angsman to the sentry and back again. Then, as he seemed about to speak, a barrel-chested brute of a man shouldered roughly through the crowd. It was Chingo.

The renegade Mimbre chief was a squat dynamo of energy, restless and quick-motioned, with a vibrant and violent nature to match. His broken face contained none of the Apache's impassiveness, being as mobile as it was cruel. His side-shuttling glance at Angsman was brief in its searing hatred; his sudden speech raged with his feeling:

"I know this white-eyes. He is Ongs-mon, a guide for the pony soldiers. He has killed Apaches with his own hand. Give him to me, Bonito. Long before I've finished with this one, he'll scream for death."

Bonito's reply was a thin and papery husking: "Chingo's thoughts are as easily read as fresh mule droppings. It is a personal thing, your hatred for this white-eyes. Why?"

Chingo scowled at this perception. "This spittle of a coyote led the pony soldiers to one of El Soldado's camps. They surprised us. My woman and my son were killed." He touched his scarred face. "This, Ongs-mon did to me himself. I swore an oath that I'd watch him die through many days and nights, that the end would come at night and his bones be scattered so that he'd walk forever between the living and the dead and find no rest." His barely suppressed passions flamed impatiently. "Now I'll do it . . . give him to me!"

"This is the one who took me alive from the white-eyed camp a sun ago," Bonito's young companion muttered, not looking at Angsman.

"Bonito is chief here, not Chingo," the old chief husked softly. "I will judge." In Spanish,

143

he said then, "Did you think that by aiding Tloh-ka you could pass safely among the Be-don-ko-he?"

"I did not think this," Angsman answered in Apache. "I meant to show that my white-eyes had come in peace."

As though he hadn't heard, Bonito piped gently on, "You thought this because you know that Tloh-ka is the son of my son."

"I did not know this," Angsman answered steadily, feeling that he stood on the shakiest ground with this wily and inscrutable old man.

Abruptly Bonito reverted to Apache: "No white-eyes I've met speaks our tongue, not even as badly as you. You have lived among the Shis-in-day."

"Yes."

"Yet you've guided the pony soldiers against us."

"This thing is true."

"You have killed Apaches."

"Yes." He felt the wicked silence of the watching Indians draw around him like an invisible net.

"Why have you come to this land, Ongs-mon, you and your white-eyes?"

Angsman began to talk quietly, starting from his meeting with the Amberleys in *Nantan* Marsden's office, carefully omitting no detail. The telling took a long while, because he spoke only in Apache, wanting to make each listener understand perfectly that his mission here was a peaceful one. Time and again he stumbled and paused in the effort to convey his thoughts without the subtle nuances of a tongue he'd never wholly mastered. Being uncivilized, his listeners were people of an abiding patience, also accustomed to long ceremonial tales, and there was no interruption. Then Chingo, champing with un-Apache restlessness, burst out, "The white-eyes' tongue splits many ways, and none are straight. When has Bonito listened to a white-eyes?"

Bonito husked tonelessly, "In this, at least, he speaks truth: he and his companions did not come for *pesh-litzog*, the yellow iron, for our scouts have told us that they found some and left it. It is Sha-be-no's white-eyes who want pesh-litzog and who whipped Tloh-ka. It is Ongs-mon who saved Tloh-ka. I have bought guns from Sha-be-no in the past; I know him. He's treacherous as a snake. Since these things are true, why should Ongs-mon lie about the rest?"

"I would put a question to Bonito," Angsman said quietly.

"I will think on whether to answer it."

"I've told you of the two white-eyes, a young one and an old one, who came to this land a summer gone, and of the strange one who wanders the canyons like a wild beast. What can Bonito tell me of these things?"

They had not seen the two white-eyes, Bonito said. They had come here before the Apaches.

145

Perhaps they were dead and their bones scattered by coyotes. Unless — Bonito paused with a good storyteller's drama, and Angsman found himself holding his breath — unless the wild man was Angsman's old one. One of Bonito's warriors who knew him had said that this old one was once a guide for the pony soldiers. They did not know how he came to be here or how his madness came on him. They hadn't harmed him, because he was already *tats-an,* though his body lived on. With scarcely a pause, Bonito's reedy murmur continued, "If you leave this land alive, you will lead no other white-eyes here."

"I will promise this."

"You'll tell none of the yellow iron here, for which white-eyes lust as starving wolves for a strayed buffalo calf."

"This too."

"You will guide no more pony soldiers against Apaches — any Apaches."

In a breath-hung instant Angsman knew how much hinged on his reply; he said steadily then, "This I will not promise."

"*Enju.* You are a man. . . . Bring out the white woman."

A big young warrior with a bluff, scowling face thrust to the front of the throng. "The white woman is mine. I ran her down and made her captive; I claim her by this."

"Who expects Matagente to lightly surrender such a claim?" Bonito's tone hinted at dry irony. He made a spare motion that broke up the

146

throng and spread it out, clearing off a space of hard-packed ground.

Laboriously the old man picked up a stick and shuffled off a slow wide circle, drawing a ring roughly fifteen feet in diameter. Then he motioned to two warriors, took their knives and laid these in the center of the circle. As the medicine man began intoning a ceremonial chant above the knives, Bonito droned quietly, "Is the meaning understood, white-eyes?"

Angsman nodded; it was the Blood Right. He would fight a duel with Matagente in the Apache fashion, for possession of the white girl.

CHAPTER TWELVE

Chingo made his loud and abusive protest. Bonito's answer was soft and dry as the rustle of dead leaves, with an irrevocable note of warning: "Matagente is of my following; his claim I've judged and decided. If the white-eyes wins against Matagente, he and the woman leave my camp alive. Then take your quarrel to him, Mimbreno. It's no concern of mine. I have spoken."

Chingo moved back to the edge of the crowd, standing scowling and spraddle-legged with arms folded, a bull-chested and dominant figure. His eyes were glazed with his frustrated hatred. He plainly feared that young Matagente might kill Angsman, cheating Chingo of the goal that centered his savage life. Bonito's reasons were equally clear: he'd evidently declared publicly that his life-long battle with the white man was ended; he was making his word firm by releasing both these white-eyes on condition. At the same time he must observe tribal justice by Matagente's claim. To Chingo, a younger upstart war chief of another tribe, he was deliberately giving short shrift, emphatically settling any doubt as to whose was the voice of command here.

The crowd gave way as a squaw approached,

pushing the stumbling white girl ahead of her. Judith Amberley's dirt-smudged face was discolored by a great swollen bruise on one cheek. Her short pale hair was matted with dirt, and her blouse was torn. Her whole slender body was slack with exhaustion and brutal treatment.

Seeing him then, she stared in unbelieving recognition. A half sob started in her throat. Almost imperceptibly Angsman shook his head; she must show no weakness. At once that still cold pride masked her face; he knew then that the iron fiber of her was untouched by what she had endured.

"Let the white-eyed woman watch," Bonito said. He turned a slow glance of grave impatience on the medicine man, who brought his muttered incantations to a hasty close.

While Angsman shed his shirt, Matagente moved into the center of the ring and stood flexing his long arms, preening for the young squaws. Watching him carefully, Angsman decided that he was not too bright and that this was Matagente's sole disadvantage. He was bigger than most of his fellows, as lean and sinewy as any. Like all Apache youths, he'd been trained from childhood for the deadliest games of close-fighting . . . his youth meant that he would think and act swiftly if not brilliantly.

Each slightly crouched, the knives on the ground between them, neither wanting to make the initial move that might give his opponent an opening. Angsman made it then, bending and scooping up his knife, leaping back before Matagente could move. He saw the brown face jerk with surprise at this unexpected reflex in a white man, one who lacked Matagente's youth by a good ten years.

Now the Apache did move, quickly dipping up his knife and pivoting away to escape Angsman's side-arcing slash at his belly. Angsman pressed him close, feinting low and then high, and Matagente, placed on a sudden defensive, retreated awkwardly. A ripple of laughter went through the crowd, and Matagente didn't like it. A soundless snarl twisted his lips and now he recovered, still retreating but with the delicate, foot-mincing shift of a trained fighter.

Angsman moved in faster; with a sudden sweep of blade he drew a fine red line across Matagente's chest, barely moving away in time. It left Angsman briefly wide open and the Apache came swiftly inside his guard, his knife arcing up and inward. Angsman grabbed his wrist, stopping the fatal thrust cold; with a savage twist he locked that arm behind Matagente's back. It might have diverted Matagente for the split-second needed for Angsman to counter-thrust, but the Apache had presence of mind enough to seize Angsman's arm as it pulled back. They strained chest to chest, Angsman fighting to turn steel into Matagente's neck, the Apache striving to free his immobilized knife-arm.

Angsman abruptly hooked his left leg around Matagente's right one and threw him, their locked bodies crashing to earth together. The white scout was on top now, his weight inching his blade nearer by straining degrees toward the Apache's throat. Matagente's body was a taut arch of resistance, tensed muscles coiled like powerful springs against every inch of his coppery hide. He succeeded in rolling them both on their sides.

Thinking always a step ahead of his slower-witted enemy, Angsman relentlessly drove his knee into Matagente's unprotected groin. Matagente twisted with agony, doubling up his knees to protect himself, and the pain galvanized him to a burst of power. He wrenched his locked arm around in front, though Angsman kept his hold.

For a time they grunted and rolled and strained, with neither gaining an advantage; their struggles carried them back to their feet. Deliberately then Angsman shifted to a wrestling position and hip-threw Matagente, at the same time releasing him. The Apache somersaulted in mid-air and hit the earth on his back with a jolting impact that knocked the wind from him. He rallied at once, kicking blindly upward, his moccasined toe slamming Angsman's hand. The knife arced from it, hit the ground and skittered among the feet of the onlookers.

Matagente bounded to his feet with a hoarse shout of triumph, moving slowly in against his opponent. Angsman shot one baffled glance at the dust-moiled spot where his knife had vanished and started a circling retreat. But there was small room for evasive tactics in this closely cordoned circle, and he had to constantly watch Matagente against a sudden charge.

There was a sudden flicker of movement — the sunflash of his knife in the dust, skidded into the ring by a sly kick. His swift glance found the face of the boy Tloh-ka, standing almost at the front of the throng. That face, not wholly disciplined in its youth, held a half-defiant vindication: whatever he owed the white man was paid in full.

Matagente, puffed with certain victory, had missed this byplay; he edged in for the kill, biding his time for a certain thrust. Suddenly Angsman darted low and past him, diving under his belated downstab of arm, hitting the ground and rolling over twice, his outflung hand closed true around the knife hilt.

Matagente's large bluff face sagged as he saw his enemy coming upright and armed; he started a desperate lunge, bearing down on Angsman before the white scout had his balance set. Angsman dug in his heels and drove in low and fast, his head butting solidly against the Apache's middle. He caught Matagente by surprise, smashing the breath from him and flopping him on his back, arms and legs thrashing wildly.

In an instant Angsman had dropped above him, his knees pinning Matagente's shoulders while his free hand caught the other's knife-wrist.

He laid his knife along the Apache's corded throat muscles.

"I give you the choice, Be-don-ko-he," he grated. "Now —"

Old Bonito's calm words were very low. "Do you choose, Matagente?"

"I — choose."

Slowly Angsman rose and stepped back; Matagente rolled onto his belly and got a knee under him, rising painfully. The pain was not physical. He turned the bald venom of his hurt on Angsman. He spat at the white man's feet and flung his knife into the spittle, spun on his heel and stalked away through the crowd. Another enemy who would not forget, Angsman knew then, thinking coldly, I should have killed him. . . .

There was a sudden flurry of confusion from the far side of the camp where the remuda grazed; the crowd broke apart, and Angsman saw a pony streaking away toward the near ridges that ended this side of the valley. A small form lay flat against its back, clinging like a burr.

Chingo voiced a fierce and raging command to his men as he spun and ran for the remuda; his five men joined him on the run. In less than a minute, the seven were riding away in hot pursuit of the escaping one.

"This is a lucky thing for you, white-eyes," old Bonito droned matter-of-factly. "While the Mimbreno is chasing down his woman, you may leave in safety. Take the white woman and go, nor come again to the lodges of the Be-don-ko-he."

After watching Angsman and the sentry vanish into the notch, Amberley and Ramirez could only lay up in the mouth of the wash and wait. James Amberley's nerves were pulled taut, and his eyes ached with the strain of staring across the heat-shimmering flat at the notch. His clothes were drenched with sweat; he could feel it pooling soddenly in his boots. He tried not to think of how thin Angsman's chances really were. . . .

"Hssst!"

The Mexican gripped his arm. Amberley heard the fast tattoo of a running horse coming up the notch and behind it what sounded like other riders in bunched pursuit.

He and Ramirez were hunched side by side behind a low barricade of rocks that partly blocked the end of the wash, and now Mexican Tom lifted his rifle from his knees and laid it across the rocks, sighting on the notch. Mechanically Amberley followed his example.

The first rider broke into sight — a small brown figure clinging bareback to a running pinto. It streaked across the flats toward the draw, covering half the distance before a half-dozen mounted bucks thundered out of the notch. And then the pinto stumbled and went down on its knees, recovered footing and lunged away. The mishap had tumbled the rider off.

It was an Indian girl, Amberley saw, climbing to her feet dazed but unhurt. She shot a glance at her horse sidling away, then at her pursuers. She began a hopeless, stumbling run toward the wash. One buck drew ahead of his fellows, grinning broadly as he quickly overhauled her.

Amberley, being a scholar and gentleman, didn't hesitate. He shot hastily at the buck and missed. The Apache wheeled his pony up short and so did his companions. The girl stopped in her tracks uncertainly. Amberley dropped his rifle, scrambled over the rocks and ran toward her, ignoring Mexican Tom's frantic, "Profes', you goddamn fool — !"

The girl shrank back now, and seeing her startled fear, Amberley slowed to a fast walk. "We're friends —" he started to call. Then the first buck, seeing a lone white man, gave a delighted whoop and kicked his pony forward.

Amberley reached the girl and pushed her behind him, tugging at his holstered revolver. The Apache thundered down on his easy prey, his slender lance poised for the thrust. Ramirez' Winchester roared. The slug wiped the buck from horseback; he hit the ground like a broken bundle of rags and rolled to a dead stop.

His cautious fellows had held back; now they broke apart, sliding to the ground and fading out of sight like dust on the rock-littered flat. Amberley put his head down and ran, dragging the girl with him. They had almost reached the rocks when the Apaches opened fire. Ramirez rapidly emptied his magazine to give them a covering fire. Amberley felt a blow in the foot that almost crossed his legs in mid-run. Then they were up and over the rocks, tumbling breathlessly down beside Ramirez.

Mexican Tom thrust the Winchester into Amberley's hands and snatched up the Easterner's ride, saying flatly, "Reload, man. Santa Maria, I think you shake down a hornets' nest on our heads."

Amberley, staring at the shot-off heel of his boot, glanced up in honest surprise. "I couldn't let them —"

"Sure, sure. Load the gun, profes', eh?" As he spoke, a buck lifted part of his body to view, ducking back with a taunting laugh as Ramirez' shot puffed rock dust from his shelter.

"This is fine game for 'Pache," Ramirez observed, rocking back on his haunches, his long brown face shining with sweat. "Well, we ain't so bad off for now. Ain't gettin' behind us without they cut across the open, makin' damn' fine target. They stuck there, we stuck here. Willie and the senorita stuck in the rancheria, and that ain't good."

Amberley turned an ashen face toward him. "Good Lord."

"Yeah. You shouldn't of been so quick to help this siwash gal, profes'. Me havin' to shoot one won't help our compadres none."

The Apaches did not shoot again, and Amberley supposed that ammunition was fairly dear to them. He glanced out once at the dead Apache, his body splayed grotesquely across the rocks and dark blood dyeing the tawny dust by his head. Amberley didn't look again, settling down to a bitter cud-chewing of self-recrimination. Then he realized that the girl was crowded tightly against him.

Mildly embarrassed, he noticed the curious plaiting of her black hair, the sturdy Apache moccasins and leggings, and the shapeless dirty cotton dress that didn't wholly conceal her youth and lithe slimness. The black eyes in her thin brown face met his with no fear now, only a deep wonderment. She smelled of grease and sweat and woodsmoke, distinct odors that badly impregnated his own clothing, he knew. He shifted uncomfortably away, muttering.

"What you say, profes'?"

"I said, what the devil will I do with a runaway Apache female!"

Ramirez briefly studied her, frowning. "I don't think this one she's Injun."

"What the devil?"

Ramirez spoke rapidly in his own language. She murmured a short reply, and he grunted. "She's Spanish, like I guess. Not much Injun blood. Mebbe none."

"I know something of your language," Amberley snapped. He was deeply irritated because he had a professional pride in his ability to identify the Latin-Indian peoples. Damned fascinating to look for traces of original Aztec or Incan bloodlines, as well as the more recent Spanish infusions. Yet now he'd been misled by first appearance, for in spite of the girl's natural darkness and deep tan, her features obviously weren't Athapascan.

Haltingly he questioned her. He learned to his vast relief that Angsman had fought and won a duel for Judith's freedom with the buck who had captured her. The girl hadn't seen more, because she had used this distraction for her first chance at escape. Of course with these warriors laid up by the notch, Angsman and Judith would have to leave the valley by another way and skirt around the notch to get here . . . which would explain their delay in coming.

The Apaches began shouting insults in Spanish, and Ramirez returned them with interest. Meanwhile Amberley questioned the girl further. She was the only daughter of Don Luis Valdez y Montalvo y Salazar y Torres, a wealthy hacendado of southern Sonora. While returning to her father's estate from a visit to relatives in Hermosillo, her small wagon party was attacked and wiped out by this same renegade band.

It appeared that the young war chief Chingo had at once conceived a strange passion for her, she reminding him of another who'd been his child-bride. Though she'd been subjected to terrible hardship in the weeks that followed, she hadn't been ill-treated or otherwise molested. Chingo, a very strange Apache, had seemed to be waiting for her heart to soften toward him.

He had used her kindly, and yet sensing something mad and twisted in the man, Pilar Torres had come to fear Chingo more than any of them.

"You're quite safe from him now," Amberley told her gently.

Her large black eyes were solemn. "I cannot say why I believe you, senor, only that I do. It must be that you're as good as you are brave."

"Oh," Amberley blushed.

A sudden crunch of gravel down the wash at their backs brought their heads around. Amberley's breath exploded from his lungs in full relief. It was Angsman and Judith. Crouching low, the two moved in to drop at their sides.

"Jude," Amberley said urgently.

"I'm fine, dear. Tired and bruised and mauled. But otherwise fine, thanks to our friend. . . ."

Angsman gave a brief nod toward the Spanish girl. "Your idea, professor?"

"What else could I do? She's not an Apache, Angsman."

"So I see. Odd she ran, though."

"What do you mean?"

"Mostly women taken by Indians, white or not, don't run away. Lot of 'em refuse to leave the tribe, offered a chance. Figure what they'll have to face with their kinfolk'll be a sight worse."

"The poor child," Judith said softly.

"Time we thought about pulling out of here."

"To where, amigo?" Mexican Tom asked

wryly. "That cabron Charbonneau is holed up in our good place."

"We'll dicker with Armand," Angsman answered grimly. "With what he's going to face, I'm thinking he'll listen."

CHAPTER THIRTEEN

When the girl Pilar mounted behind Judith Amberley, the five people began their slow retreat down the wash, Angsman and Ramirez bringing up a rear guard. Angsman knew that Chingo and his men would follow, well out of sight. An Apache wasn't supposed to attack until all odds ran his way, but trying to graft hard-and-fast rules on the behavior of a maverick like Chingo was to run yourself up a blind alley. The young Mimbreno's mind and motives were too twisted and unpredictable, and he had three good reasons not to rest until he'd settled with this party of white-eyes: Ramirez had killed one of his handful of loyal followers, Amberley had snatched away his prize captive, and Angsman, his blood enemy, was one of them.

The shadows had lengthened when they dropped wearily off the rugged heights before the final swing down to Obregon Pass. On a rare wide stretch of rolling dunes and flats where they could see for a mile in any direction, Angsman called a brief halt, to give horses and riders a safe breather.

Almost at once Chingo and his followers appeared on a distant bare ridge and likewise dismounted. Five of them dropped from their mounts and hunkered down to rest and watch, but the sixth man felt frisky. He abandoned his loincloth and exposed his hindquarters, strutting back and forth as he made obscene and taunting gestures at the whites.

"What *is* he doing?" Judith Amberley burst out. A little later she turned away, her face scarlet. "Well — *really!*"

Angsman rubbed his chin thoughtfully. "That my Winchester you're hefting, Tomas?"

"Si, amigo. She's a repeater, and I was usin' her to pin down them cabrons back there — you want her?"

"No. I was wondering where's your old Army Springfield. Singleshot, but it's got a mite better range than my long gun."

A broad grin of understanding broke Ramirez' long face. "I get her." He went to his horse and got the battered rifle from its boot. Angsman took it, checked the load, then stretched out on his belly behind a low flat rock. He laid the barrel across it and began to place his aim, calculating windage and angle. He drew a slow breath, held it, and squeezed off his shot. The cavorting buck, standing sideways, leaped as though stung; he ran a few queer, bucking steps, holding his buttocks, then rolled wildly on the ground.

Mexican Tom whooped his delight, and Angsman rose to his feet with a faint grin, handing back the rifle. He would have tried for Chingo, but couldn't identify the war chief at this distance. The lucky long shot had its immediate effect; the Apaches realized they weren't quite out of rifle range and scrambled back over the ridge, dragging their horses and their floundering fellow with them. That, Angsman judged with satisfaction, should pull Chingo off for a while. He had already lost one man, and another would be riding no warpaths for a time. His force was cut to three, very un-Apache odds.

An hour later they left the last heights and followed a branch canyon which brought them to the terminus of Obregon Pass below Muro del Sangre, here pausing to debate their next move. Both Amberleys were cool to Angsman's idea of joining forces with Armand Charbonneau; they'd had altogether enough of that unscrupulous gentleman, Judith declared flatly. Angsman pointed out that Charbonneau and his crew were forted up in their own choice cul-de-sac, the best place he'd found to withstand an attack.

Sooner or later, he added, Chingo would be raging down on their trail. It might take time for the Mimbreno to recruit help from his hostile fellow Apaches, Bonito's tribesmen, but eventually he could probably persuade a number of the younger Chiricahua bucks to follow him. They would be champing restlessly from months of inactivity in the rancheria, their savage spirits hardly allayed by the little hunting available here. A small park of whites in their own country was their natural prey. Old Bonito had restrained them so far, but Chingo could wear through that thin checkrein by persuasion and by wondering aloud whether all Chiricahuas were women.

James Amberley frowned. "But I thought Bonito more or less agreed. . . ."

"Bonito's quit fighting. That goes for those who'll follow his lead. But every Apache warrior's his own man, professor. Even the hereditary chiefs are really sort of sage senior advisers. Most times the rest will follow 'em, if only because most people like to be led. But Bonito's not even a hereditary leader. He's a war chief, an ordinary warrior with extra status on a war party: that's when he gives orders and the rest listen. To his people, Bonito's come to mean a good deal more — a sort of living symbol of what they once were — and he's a sound leader in his own right. But he's got no legal power as tribal law recognizes it. Chingo's descended from old Tah-zay, a famous Mimbreno chief; he's got that edge. Also, the younger bucks looked up to Bonito because he was the most warlike of 'em all. Now he's hung up his fighting spurs, he's going to lose something in the eyes of the feisty ones. Chingo may be a mite crazy, but he's smart enough to know all this."

It was a long speech for Angsman, and now he paused before adding pointedly: "We got a couple days' grace maybe, while he's rallying his young men. But he'll come sure as sunrise. When he does, we'll be sitting ducks, unless we do two things: we find a good fort and we throw

164

in with Charbonneau. That's three more guns, and we'll need 'em all."

Amberley sighed. "Your argument seems unassailable, and I suppose there's no alternative?"

"Just one, professor."

"What's that?"

"We use the time that's left to pack up and clear out," Angsman replied flatly. As he spoke, his gaze veered hard and direct to Judith Amberley. She flushed, but he knew from the immediate stubborn set of her thin, smudged and sunburned face that on this point she wouldn't yield a jot.

"Not," she said clearly, coldly, "until we have learned of Douglas."

Angsman merely nodded, then gigged his horse down the pass. By now the muted glow of sunset was shedding its refulgence across the rim, dyeing the walls to a soft gray-blue, and deep shadows began to fill the canyon vales. Enough light remained to make out shape if not detail, and now Angsman caught a shadow of movement in the mouth of a side canyon.

Instantly he spurred his mount sideward toward it, and a dark form sprang up and started a hobbling run. Angsman let his horse out, plunging recklessly into the canyon and bearing swiftly down on the figure. It wheeled to face him; he glimpsed a snarling face half-hidden by a tangle of white hair and beard, thin arms raising a heavy knob stick.

Angsman reined his horse to a skidding halt, roughly swinging the animal so that its shoulder slammed the man's scrawny chest, knocking his light body spinning. He sprawled face down and didn't move. Angsman vaulted to the ground and threw his reins. It was their wild man, for sure. Angsman stooped above him, wary that he might be shamming, and then saw the blood trickling from a deep cut in the man's scalp where his head had struck a rock in falling. He turned the wild man on his back. It took him a full five seconds to identify positively Caleb Tree, the old guide from Fort Stambaugh.

Behind his filthy matted hair and beard, Tree's bony features were ravaged by privation — and something worse. His feet were bare, horny and calloused, and his bare arms and legs were withered sticks, the weathered skin taut across bone and tendon. Only tattered dirty rags remained of his clothing.

The others moved up slowly, and Amberley murmured, "Good God." The others said nothing, watching Angsman feel for pulse and heartbeat. He looked up at Judith Amberley, answering the question in her strained dark gaze.

"He's alive — Bonito had it right."

"Caleb Tree," she whispered.

Angsman nodded, dropping his gaze to the unconscious man. Whatever hope there was of discovering Douglas Amberley's fate lay locked in the maniacal brain of this half-starved bundle of bones and skin, and looking at him now,

Angsman thought that hope was pretty thin. He did not voice his pessimism, coming now to his feet.

"Best we don't move him. Make him comfortable as you can and keep a sharp eye on him. Crazy man is wilier than most. Rest of you stay here while I see friend Armand."

Mexican Tom stood hipshot, thumbs tucked in his belt and his Springfield slung in the crotch of his arm. "Better you don't go alone, amigo."

Angsman shook his head. "You stay. This calls for talk, and I talk Charbonneau's language. No love lost, but we understand each other from way back."

He left them, hiking downcanyon through the pooling shadows, following the stream a half-mile and swinging with it into the branch canyon. He paced noiselessly up the pebbly bank to where the dark mouth of the cul-de-sac yawned, lifting his voice:

"Charbonneau!"

No answer. From here Angsman could see the orange wash of firelight bathing the inner wall of the ravine, and he said in a normal tone and drily, "All right, Armand. I'm alone. One man come to scare hell out of you."

A tall lean form detached itself from a bulge of shadow and came forward, halting a cautious dozen feet away. The faint light laid blue glints along a rifle barrel.

"One thing I nevair figure you for, Angsman, is a great fool."

"You're a sight too smart to shoot before you hear me out, Armand."

"That is very true." The Creole's white grin was wolfish. "Not till I know whether there's anythin' in it for Armand, eh? We figure you are dead . . . the othairs too."

"No thanks to you we aren't. Kincaid, though. . . ."

"You?"

" 'Paches."

Charbonneau lowered the rifle with an expressive shrug. "He was a fool. What 'appen?"

Angsman explained, and then Charbonneau doubled his long legs and settled on his haunches, rifle across his knees, thoughtfully stroking his beard. "Thing about a deal is, a man has something to give, something to get. You need our fort, our guns. W'at you got to give, Will?"

Angsman sank down facing him. Idly, he scooped up a handful of sand and sifted it through his fingers, saying softly, "Use your head, Armand. The 'Paches know you're here. Bonito paid you back for that whipped kid when his braves got Kincaid; that score's settled. He wants no more trouble with whites. Fact remains that when Kincaid and Staples whipped Bonito's grandson, they cut clean any understandings you and him had once. You're on your own now with Chingo set to rampage. We'll be camped on your doorstep, and when Chingo's through with us, he'll just be cutting his teeth. Afterward there'll be you. None of us'll leave the Toscos alive that way." He added wryly, " 'We must hang together, or most assuredly we shall hang separately.' "

"Huh," Charbonneau grunted. "Ben Franklin, ain't it? You know, Will, I'm of good family in N'Orleans. Called myself an educated man, once. Never thought of you as one, though."

"We'll compare family notes sometime," Angsman told him drily, feeling a faint irritation. He had never hinted of his past to any of his Western acquaintances, and he realized that in some obscure way he might have been on guard against doing so. Maybe he'd used up the reason for that self-restraint. The thought passed fleetingly across his mind, and then he said: "We're three able-bodied men; with your three, that's six. A sight better odds. How's it to be, Armand? I haven't got all night."

Charbonneau shifted on his heels to get out a cheroot, placed his thumbnail to a match and paused. "You say Chingo pull' back?"

"For the time."

"Good — so I don't give them red riggers no target." Charbonneau snapped the match alight; its saffron flare highlighted his roughly debonair features as he lighted his cheroot. Puffing, he said, "Three and two makes five, Will."

"How you mean?"

Charbonneau was silent a moment. He tossed

the match away with a deep sigh. "The kid, Will-John . . . he die this morning." His tone became musing. "He was a fonny kid . . . a little crazy in the head with wantin' to make his fortune. Just an Ohio farm boy, you comprehend, who leave his girl and come to the great West where a man can make money overnight, enough to buy a fine big farm where he can be proud to bring his Lucy. But a kid like that, not very bright, slow like an ox, what is there for him anywhere but the hard labor?"

"Or making a big fast killing by throwing in with cutthroats?"

Charbonneau's shoulders heaved in a chuckle. "You anticipate me, mon ami. Maybe I feel sorry for the kid, maybe them big brown eyes remind me of a poodle my grandmere give me once. Anyway, I like him, I take him on. Figure first big job that comes off, I send him packin' back to his Lucy with a bonus. Enough to get marry, buy that farm, raise a brood of towheaded slow-witted brats." The cherry-coal of the cheroot glowed brightly as he drew on it. "An' now all that is left of poor Will-John an' his dreams is buried under a pile of rock back in this cul-de-sac. Damn' fonny how things work sometime . . . I kind of like that kid."

"I know how heartbroken you must be. It a deal or not?"

"Ah oui, why not? I am feel' generous; 'ave my next-to-last cheroot, we smoke on it."

"We don't have to smoke on it," Angsman

told him curtly. "It's a truce, Armand. If we get out of this, I'll be watching my back with you. That's one thing never changes where you're concerned."

CHAPTER FOURTEEN

Two days passed in the cul-de-sac. The time of grace left before Chingo made his move was narrowing, if Angsman was right . . . the Mimbreno might have already assembled his force and was waiting on the chance that he might catch one or all of them in the open. But Angsman doubted it: Chingo had none of the infinite patience of his people. His great nemesis was his own seething energy; it couldn't be bridled for long.

Meanwhile, with five men to alternate the guard duty, they were all left with a good deal of time on their hands. Charbonneau, Ambruster and Tom Ramirez used it to gather some of the float gold that enriched the nearby stream, working out daily from the cul-de-sac. They thoroughly covered the branch canyon and even worked a short distance up Obregon Pass, but none of them ventured too far. The three men panned for the yellow metal from dawn to dusk; all were exhausted but feverishly exuberant at the end of the second day. Already each had a heavy poke containing several hundred dollars worth of dust.

Strangely, Angsman found himself unaffected by their fever. True, though he'd found prospecting a fair means of grubstaking his long desert sojourns, it had never been an addicted lust with him as with some prospectors. Still under ordinary circumstances he'd have availed himself of this opportunity, as would any normal man. He supposed that his present indifference was part of facing this turning point in his life and not being yet certain of what direction it was taking.

He spent the hours studying himself, on his past and present, on life in general, and mostly on the people around him with whom he'd become peculiarly involved. He guessed that one other who might be changing was James Amberley. The staid Easterner was plainly entranced with the Spanish girl he had rescued; he spent hours sitting with her out of earshot of the others, quietly talking. Angsman wondered amusedly what a man like Amberley, scholarly and reserved to shyness, in whose life there had obviously been no woman except his mother and sister, could find to speak of with a young girl . . . but he seemed to be having no trouble.

With the pliancy of youth, Pilar Torres had swiftly recovered from her harsh and frightening weeks as the prisoner of renegade Apaches. She still wore the ragged dress and Apache moccasins, but through some woman's wizardry she no longer resembled a thin, frightened waif. She was quite pretty with her vivacious play of dark eyes and smiling lips, and often the soft trill of her laughter welcomely broke the grim quiet.

Because she was quick of wit and speech and fully understood their danger, Angsman had guessed that her high spirits were due to her escape from Chingo. Later, becoming more aware of her bright-eyed attention to the professor, he concluded that Pilar had a private happiness of her own.

Of this, Angsman guessed that Judith Amberley had taken a dim view from the outset. But she had occupied herself in caring for Caleb Tree, rarely leaving his side. Something obsessive in her tender concern worried Angsman . . . she had hardly eaten or slept for two days and nights. How far did she intend carrying this thing?

The old man had taken complete leave of his senses, spending hours in raving delirium, becoming so violent that he had to be held down. Angsman guessed that the head blow Tree had taken only partly explained his condition. They'd found a badly healed scar on his scalp which must have been inflicted months ago. Afterward, already aged to senility and living like an animal, he'd received none of the proper care and rest which might have restored him. Angsman hoped for Judith's sake that Tree might come to his right senses, at least briefly. It might be better if she never learned the truth, but how could a man judge? It was certain that she couldn't go on with the blind spot of Douglas' fate gnawing in her mind.

A few years back when the Army, constantly

in the field against the insurgent Apaches, had required a large contingent of civilian scouts, Angsman had been chief of scouts at Fort Stambaugh for a time. He'd made it his business to know his men, Caleb Tree among them. The ancient mountain man had always been irascible, reserved to taciturnity, and it was said that he'd had liaison between gun-runners and Sioux-Arapahoe in the Dakota campaigns, though nothing was proved. Such talk was current through the army echelons, and Major Marsden had passed it on to Angsman as a word of precaution. Angsman had decided that Tree was capable of nearly anything, but was too shrewd to be caught out. He was thoroughly reliable aside from that; his knowledge of the territory he'd ranged from the early fur-trapping and trading days was second to none.

From this meager knowledge and Tree's near-incoherent ravings now, Angsman had tried to piece together what might have happened after he and young Amberley had left Fort Stambaugh. But the old man had only carped on happenings that were now frontier legend, confirming what Angsman had supposed: Tree's past contained dark spots that no man in his right senses would reveal.

Pondering all of it as he sat off to one side on the evening of the second day, Angsman decided that only time could fill out the answers. He glanced at the others, picked out by flickering firelight. Ramirez was on guard at the entrance of the cul-de-sac. Caleb Tree's sleeping form was bundled in blankets by the fire. He'd been resting well for some hours now, his wasted chest rising and falling with steady breathing. Amberley and Pilar sat away from the others, their voices bare murmurs. Turk Ambruster was carrying on an awkward conversation with Judith, while Charbonneau sat cross-legged by the fire; his teeth clamped a dead stub of cheroot while he scowled over the contents of his gold poke which he had spilled out on a blanket, muttering under his breath in French.

Gold fever's really got Armand, Angsman thought narrowly. There's another it'll do to watch. . . .

". . . But Mr. Lincoln freed the slaves, Mr. Ambruster," Judith was asserting earnestly, as she sat facing the big Negro, her knees drawn up to her chin.

"Yes'm," Ambruster rumbled patiently. "But that didn't make no never mind to a black man in the south, even after Genril Lee surrendered. You don't write off folks' feelin's by signin' no paper. You was a 'Bolitionist, ma'am? Lots of Massachusetts folks was."

"My father was," Judith smiled.

"Sure, you'd of been a little gal then. What I'm sayin', you folks never saw they ain't no easy answers. Us people wasn't ready for freedom when it bust on us overnight. They was carpetbaggers who used us while we went plumb wild. An' that reconstruction was hard on the white

South'ners, made 'em bitter. You ast how I wound up out here with a renegade bunch. Details ain't so important as the whys an' wherefores. Easy to set blame without thinkin' it through. We's all to blame, come down to it. Hope I ain't offended you, ma'am."

"You are an intelligent and discerning man, sir, and I'm afraid that my ignorance is an insult to you."

Ambruster smiled widely. "No, ma'am, I'm pleased for your interest. I been playin' a mean dumb bad actor so long, I just —"

"Turk." Charbonneau spoke flatly, without looking up. "How you think it looks, eh, you talkin' to this white ma'mselle?"

All the diehard arrogance of a dead way of life tinged his words, and Judith replied angrily, "How dare you! I will speak to whomever I please, and so will he!"

"No, ma'am," Ambruster rumbled softly, coming to his feet. "Things as they are, Armand's right. Was right nice talkin' to you . . . man could forgit for a little while. Anyways I got to look to my horse."

"I will not press you, sir, but you are always welcome to speak to me."

"Thank you." Ambruster turned away toward the niche where their horses were tethered on the patch of grass. He paused. "Figgered oncet I had a bellyful of knowtowin' to white folk, servin' 'em, only —" he hesitated "— anythin' I can ever do fer you, miss, you whistle."

He walked quickly away.

Judith sighed, then bent above Caleb Tree, tucking the blankets closely under his chin, afterward rising to her feet and walking over to where Angsman sat with his back propped against a rock, legs outstretched and crossed, slacked at complete rest with the negligent ease of a big cat. She settled her own back to the rock a few feet away, her face softly brooding. "How terrible. You would think that among outlaws, at least, a man might enjoy freedom from the barrier of his skin color."

Angsman said nothing, and she added sharply, "Of course you're Southern."

"Don't bait me, lady," he murmured. "Your Pa was likely a merchant. Mine owned a big Virginia farm — owned four slaves. We lost everything when McClellan went through to Richmond. Took years to recover. Man can't wipe his memory clean like a kid's slate. As your friend said, there's no easy answer."

"Then," she said icily, "you think —"

"Tom Ramirez is my friend. I've lived with Mexicans, Indians. That answer you?"

"I'm sorry," she said wearily, pressing a hand to her temple. "I'm tired and upset. This danger . . . caring for the old man . . . and then Jimmy and that girl —"

"Different when it touches you, eh?"

"Certainly not," she snapped. "Anyway she's really a Spaniard, not a Mexican. But she's been with those Apaches. You haven't lived away from society so long that you've forgotten how people talk."

"That matter?"

"It does, and don't deny it. You have to live with other people, however you dislike their thinking."

"And with yourself."

"That is no answer."

"It is for me."

"It's selfish."

"Leastways I don't try living someone else's life."

"What a cruel thing to say!"

"Sorry. None of my business."

"Perhaps it is. You've certainly earned the right to know." She was silent a moment, biting her lip. "Try to understand. Though Jimmy's older than me, I've had to look after him constantly since our parents died. Somebody had to . . . he's so impractical. He paid no attention to girls when he was younger, and he's always been tied up in his work. Now he's swept quite off his feet by this girl. It simply won't work. Can you blame me for being concerned?"

"Boston's a long way off. No reason anyone has to know about the Apache business. He met her in the southwest — that's all."

She laughed bitterly. "How very simple. A strange little waif of a girl —"

"The daughter of a grandee. Her people likely set foot on American soil before yours did. She'll stand head and shoulders in Boston society —

even be the rage of your class for a time."

"Rather good, for a desert-dweller," she said mockingly. "But her religion does place strong conditions on marriage. You see? That's the sort of thing poor Jim never thinks of."

Angsman smiled. "I've talked some to this little lady. Have the feeling that won't make a jot of difference to her."

"But she's only a child — Jim is thirty-four. At least fifteen years difference. Oh, it's impossible!"

"Wouldn't know. Never made up other people's lives as I went along. Too selfish, I reckon."

She stiffened icily, then relaxed with a sigh. "Perhaps you're right. Perhaps I am only making excuses to hold onto him at any cost. There were only the three of us . . . and Douglas is gone. And yet I lost him because —" She shook her head, her eyes haunted. "Never mind. At least it should have taught me a lesson. Perhaps I'm generically a meddling fool."

"You can be too hard on yourself too."

Her glance was quick and a little surprised. It was the first gentle word he had given her, Angsman realized with a faint nudge of shame. The desert hardened and roughened a man farther than skin-deep; whatever wells of gentleness remained were almost buried.

"Strange — I just realized that you hadn't breathed a word of your past until you mentioned your father's farm — in Virginia. Is that all?"

He shrugged bleakly. "The rest isn't important."

"Perhaps it is."

He turned his head and met her eyes fully, saying after a moment, "Maybe sometime I'll. . . ."

They heard a low moan over by the fire. Caleb Tree had elbowed himself to a sitting position, and was staring vacantly about. "Where's this child at?" His faded eyes came to sharp focus under a frosty rim of brows. "That you, Angsman?"

"Me, Cal." Angsman went down on one knee by the old man while Judith on his other side pushed Caleb Tree firmly back. He glared at her. Angsman shook his head slightly and she drew back, biting her lip.

"Hoss, who's thet thin biddy?"

"She's cared for you mighty close, Caleb," Angsman said gently. "Been out of your head a long time."

"Know that," Caleb Tree grunted testily, gingerly passing a scrawny hand over his white hair. "Took a knock on the head. Was quite a spell ago. Some of it comin' back. Not all. What'n hell happent?"

"Remember Doug Amberley?" Angsman studied Tree's face as he spoke.

Just a couple of days' rest seemed to have begun restoring the old man. The second head injury he'd sustained might even have helped his memory and sanity — Angsman had heard of such things. Anyway he was rational enough for the moment. This might be a good time, while his recollection remained murky, to try to catch him off-guard on any subterfuge he'd attempt.

Caleb Tree swept the circle of intent faces with a shuttling glance, coming back to Angsman's. "Amberley. Young cub I brought here. I 'member. A little, leastways . . . ain't too clear."

"The kid's dead, Cal."

Judith gasped, and Angsman ignored her, watching for Tree's reaction. Tree's eyes narrowed. "Could be so, hoss," he murmured.

He wouldn't be baited into self-betrayal, Angsman knew then, and told himself, Go easy now. Aloud he said quietly, "How much you remember?"

Haltingly, pausing many times to knit his white brows, the mountain man told them of bringing Douglas Amberley to this place, of finding the old Spanish gold diggings and making camp there. Of sighting the cave entrance high on the pass wall, where the Obregon party had taken refuge . . . and of finding a way to reach it. "My stick don't float no further, hoss — she's hung on a snag. Cub wanted to look in them caves . . . all I know."

Angsman told him, "Take your time," his glance touching Judith then. She was gnawing her lip, hands clasping her knees with white-knuckled fingers. "You sure about the cave, old timer? I spotted it myself. But if there was ever a trail up there, it's gone."

"Wagh. Know that." Tree hesitated, frowning. " 'Member now. Didn't come to it from b'low. Follered thet big slide up to the rim, let ourse'f down by rope. Wa'n't nohow easy, but. . . ." He broke off, a fleeting wariness touching his seamed face in its filthy tangle of white hair and beard. Angsman knew then that Tree's own words had surfaced some troubled memory. Angsman gave him no chance to backtrack, pressing it mercilessly: "Let's have it . . . then?"

Tree's tongue rimmed his cracked lips. "Wagh," he grunted irascibly. "Tryin', hoss. Give an old man time."

"What happened?"

Tree's white head stirred in vague negation. "Damn this child's liver an' lights if he kin recollect. . . ."

Whatever Tree's reason for being evasive, Angsman knew that at last they had pinpointed something certain. "Reckon we can make it down to those caves same way you did," he said softly.

To that Tree said nothing, closing his eyes. Shortly he seemed to be asleep.

"Tomorrow, Angsman," Judith Amberley's voice was coldly even, "you and I will go together."

About to flatly state that he'd go alone, Angsman hesitated. Getting to the caves could prove dangerous, but she'd never settle this thing with herself until she saw whatever was to be seen with her own eyes. He nodded curtly. "Get your sleep. There'll be some hard climbing."

Angsman was not sure what woke him . . . it might have been a mere shadow of sound. He came awake at once, every sense alert, as was his habit. A crouched form was half-bent above him, and he had an instant to register a wicked flash of firelight on knife before he rolled, sidelong and away, his legs tangled in his blanket. The tail of his eye caught the last of that livid steel arc as it ended in his ground sheet, ripped savagely through the tough tarp, yanked free. A wiry form veered away in a hobbling run.

Angsman lunged from the ground, tearing a foot free of his blanket, landing with a grunt on his side as his hand closed around a bony ankle. With surprising strength Tree dragged him a foot before turning with a curse, his knife lifted. Angsman twisted savagely and Tree's light frame turned in the air and fell on its back. Angsman reached for a higher grip, took it in a fistful of Tree's ragged shirt. His other hand caught a skinny wrist, twisting till the knife fell free. He kicked free of his blanket and got up, dragging Tree into the ruddy glare of the fire.

Mexican Tom, drawn by the commotion, hurried up from his guard post. "All right, Tomas. It's under control." Angsman glanced at the others rolling out of their blankets, and again at Tree. His ancient shrunken body was hunched in a tight crouch, bearing the force of his hate against them all.

His attempt on Angsman's life merely confirmed suspicion: Tree's memory had fully returned with its knowledge of what they would find in the cave. He'd shrewdly feigned weakness and sleep, waiting till they slept to make his break, not knowing about Ramirez on guard outside the cul-de-sac. He had stealthily filched a sleeper's knife to make his try for the guide before his escape, knowing that only Angsman could track him down later.

Angsman hefted the knife lightly in his palm, saying, "Think this is yours, Armand," before tossing it to Charbonneau. The Creole snaked it deftly out of the air by the hilt, sheathed it with a cool nod. "Feisty old *bastard*, ain't he?"

"This child 'ud of killed you, Angsman!" Tree shrilled suddenly. "I'd 'a sliced your sweetbreads outen your goddam plew!"

"That's right, Caleb," Angsman said slowly. "So you're going with us tomorrow. Might be you can show us what you're afraid we'll find up in that cliff."

CHAPTER FIFTEEN

On foot the three of them left the cul-de-sac shortly after first light — the scout, the woman, and the old mountain man. They headed up Obregon Pass, hugging the right wall. Here a litter of heavy boulders fallen from the rim would lend plentiful cover at a moment's notice. Angsman was held back by Judith, helping her over the roughest places. Caleb Tree hobbled ahead of them, his tattered trousers flapping around his thin muscle-knotted shanks, his calloused feet impervious to the flinty ground.

Angsman had left him tied hand and foot last night after the attempt at escape, drawing the ropes mercilessly tight. At first barely able to walk, the old man was now swinging briskly along. He hadn't uttered a word since last night.

"I feel guilty," Judith whispered. "Look at him . . . poor old man. I can't help feeling —"

"Don't," Angsman cut in quietly. "Don't deceive yourself. He's tough as rawhide, in mind and body. He's only watching for a chance to get out of this with a whole skin, even if he has to kill both of us to do it."

"As he probably killed Doug!"

"We don't know that. Best to go slow." He was considering the possibility that Chingo and his bucks might come before they returned to the cul-de-sac; if that happened, they would be cut off from the others. Angsman had flatly argued against Amberley's first insistence on accompanying them. No sense to jeopardize any more lives. If Chingo came, the cul-de-sac would have to be defended. And, Angsman had pointed out, there was Pilar. The reminder had clinched Amberley's reluctant agreement.

Reaching the broad slide where the cliff had long ago collapsed, they started upward. It was a rugged climb to the rim, and all three were breathing heavily when they reached it. Swinging east along the cliffs, Angsman held them to a cautious advance. The rimrock was weathered and rotten, and from the debris below, it must have often scaled away in great chunks . . . the slightest jar might start a slide.

They halted above the flinty ribbon of ledge. It lay about thirty feet below the rim. Angsman had been prepared for the difficult descent of an almost sheer drop, for so it appeared from the bottom. He saw now that the rim actually sloped off at a steep angle down to a slight shelf above the cave mouth. He had come lightly geared and provisioned, taking only a canteen of water and a pocketful of jerked beef, together with his pistol and rifle, some candles Amberley had thoughtfully packed, and two ropes coiled over his shoulder.

The descent to the ledge should be relatively simple — the danger lay in the badly eroded rim and the wall immediately below the rim. It appeared that this whole upper cliff had become badly faulted; a slight disturbance might cause it to plunge at any time.

Of this he said nothing, slipping the ropes from his shoulders and uncoiling them. Holding an end of each, he let them snake down to the ledge. Their fifty-foot lengths reached with plenty of slack to spare. He hauled them up and selected a huge rough-sided boulder back off the rim, knotting an end of each line securely around it. He tied one opposite end around Judith's waist, the other beneath her arms, then tested the knots. The tying up had taken a good deal of slack, but enough remained to make the ledge.

"Go down backward," he told her. "Don't think about it and don't look down. Think of doing a Sunday promenade walking backward." She smiled, and then he said a little awkwardly, "Don't be frightened. There's me, and just in case, the boulder."

Her gray eyes were steady. "I won't be frightened."

Keeping a watchful eye on Tree, Angsman braced himself on the rim and gripped the rope two-handed, gradually letting it out as she went over the rim, her feet feeling out each step of the rough slant. She tightly fisted the upper rope and kept her eyes up, not looking down as Angsman must. He felt the sweat start on his forehead, seeing her framed against the dizzy drop. She reached the shelf above the cave, let herself carefully over it, and Angsman lowered her slowly the last few feet.

On the ledge Judith pried the knots loose with the tip of her knife, freeing herself from the ropes. Angsman murmured, "Well, Caleb, you too old to shinny down?"

Tree sent him a stare of bleak hatred, then snorted softly, grabbed both ropes and clambered down the slant with a kind of stiff agility that made Angsman smile. When Tree had nearly reached the ledge, he himself made a swift descent, dropping to Tree's side in a few seconds.

Judith had already moved into the cave mouth, peering against its darkness, and he moved over to her, shoving Tree ahead of him. He took one of the short thick candles from his pocket, struck a match and handcupped the flame. The wick took it easily in the musty still air, and now with its sickly washback of shadow, he saw a deep cavern penetrating back into the cliff. Propelling Caleb Tree ahead, he picked his way over the rubbled floor, Judith's fingers tight around his arm. The tunnel walls had an angular jaggedness, and Angsman guessed that it was a mere fault formed by an ancient convulsion, later handhewn to its present rugged proportions by some prehistoric tenants. The work must have involved years of patient labor, breaking and chipping with crude flint tools; only the rottenness of the rock would have made it possible. To those primitive people, the result had no doubt been worth it: a secure fortress-home against the dangers of their savage world.

At long intervals, internal faults similarly hewn into negotiable passages intersected the main tunnel, sometimes penetrating it through floor or ceiling, so that the place was a labyrinth. Angsman swore under his breath; it could make their search near-hopeless. A man could spend days trying to trace out this maze and never find his way out. Which was why he'd brought Caleb Tree — as a last measure he could force the old man to talk. For now, there was no danger of becoming lost while they held to this main shaft . . . might as well follow it out.

Now it cut hard to the left on a flinty downslope, and they groped along cautiously, the saffron flame bathing out the walls ahead, those behind slipping back into oblivion. Angsman had thought he was inured to every sort of harsh exigency, but for an outdoorsman, this business of crawling through the ground like a damned mole was different. Something about it laid a suffocating tension against a man. Maybe it was some aroused racial memory of a time when men had believed in trolls that lived in the recesses of the earth. For a while he had to fight the urge to scramble up to sunlight and fresh air.

Shortly the roof and sides of the tunnel sharply rose, and they stepped into a vaulted round chamber, this obviously hollowed out by human hands. The candlelight played over a high roof of reddish brown crumbling rock, with odd patches of deep blackening. Soot and smoke above the sites of cooking fires, he guessed, and then held the candle lower. Judith gasped — the light played on the partly intact skeletons of animals, horses from their skulls. The slaughtered ponies of Obregon and his party, but where was the gold they had carried here?

"Angsman," Judith whispered.

"Wait," he said slowly. "Can't be a dead end. . . ." He circled the chamber, holding the light near the floor. With his toe he unearthed a half-buried object — a stone metate. And other relics. A flint arrowhead, a fragment of yucca matting, shards of broken pottery on which the black-on-white paint designs seemed almost fresh. And something else — bits of whitened stone, soft and crumbling to the touch. He blew the dry powder of what had been human bone from his hand and straightened up.

Time had almost stood still in this place, yet that fact lent a sense of incredible ancientness. Ages ago people had been here. They had birthed and lived and died, leaving some of their possessions almost intact, and yet their own substance was now dust a man could blow from his palm. It had an effect both serene and unsettling, giving a man the kind of thoughts he couldn't stay with for long.

Caleb Tree's voice, cracked and dry and broken by hollow echoes, startled him. "Wanta find young Amberley, do you, hoss?"

Angsman eyed him narrowly, wondering at his sly, humorous calm.

"Oh, please," Judith whispered. "If you know anything. . . ."

"Know a sight, missy. Studyin' on whether to tell you." Tree stroked his dirty beard with a malicious grin, and Angsman supposed he was savoring his peculiar advantage here in some twisted way.

"Caleb," he said quietly, "don't push it now."

"Don't you, child. Fer I'll tell you this: 'thout old Cal, you ain't gonna find a billy-be-damned thing. I fixed that."

His faded eyes alight with childish pleasure cut swiftly from one to the other. Abruptly, then: "I done my studyin'. Looka here." He hobbled across the chamber to a large slab tilted against the wall, seemingly inset there. He seized on it, saying testily, "Lay hold, hoss."

Angsman joined him, and together they dragged the stone outward at an angle till it tilted and crashed on its side. A low black maw was exposed. Tree grunted, muttering, "Ain't got the stren'th I had when I laid that thing agin it."

"After you," Angsman said softly.

Tree bared his yellow teeth in a grin and ducked into the opening. Angsman reached his hand to Judith and she took it, following him at a low crouch through the tight burrow. They emerged into a second chamber larger than the first, of which their entrance was one of several passages intersecting it. A draft caught the candle flame; it guttered low and Angsman cupped his hand about it, holding his breath till its sallow flicker grew.

Tree was chuckling softly; there was a tense mad fiber to the sound that made Angsman's spine crawl. Judith pressed trembling against his arm as he held the candle low. The light caught on a dull yellow glitter. Gold bars stacked against a wall. A fortune in bullion deserted by the Spaniards in their last desperate try for escape. Ten full *cargas* of six bars each, molded in the old Spanish way to cylinders two and a half feet long and six inches thick.

Tree knelt by the stacked metal, his clawed trembling hands fumbling across it, shaken by his quiet chortling. Angsman watched him a cold moment, then turned away, moving deeper into the chamber.

Judith, clinging to him, screamed softly.

The skeleton at their feet was that of a man. The grinning empty-socketed skull was still encased in a helmet of hammered brass; the fleshless ribs still wore a corroded steel breastplate. Rotten leather harness clung to it here and there. Beneath the pelvic bones lay a straight sword of what had been Spanish steel, partly drawn from its metal scabbard and rusted there as the arrested motion of a long-dead hand had left it.

"One man," Angsman said, his voice hollow and quiet, "was killed here, when they fought over their last provisions. The old Don told it straight all the way."

He moved farther along the wall. Judith's breathing was steady in his ear, but he could feel her leashed tension biting at his own nerves. And then they found the second skeleton, twisted as it had fallen in its dying sprawl. In this deep dry air, the bones of dead men looked much the same till they began falling to dust, whether they were fleshless a year or two hundred years. But this one's clothing was still whole, faded and sunken against the skeletal ridges and cavities.

Judith said tonelessly, "I gave Doug that belt . . . for his birthday." She seemed to be standing in a shocked trance, and then she sank down on her knees with a low moan. Angsman reached a hand to her shoulder . . . he stiffened with a swift backward glance.

Caleb Tree was gone.

Angsman stooped and jabbed his candle upright into the sand floor. He crouched there, his gun in hand, listening — he heard nothing. Tree had slipped silently away into one of the converging tunnels, and now Angsman knew why he'd shown them the chamber which he'd painstakingly blocked off: to provide this momentary distraction.

Angsman dug out another candle and lighted it, thinking coolly against his sense of warning urgency. Tree would try escape by the way they had come, rather than risk losing himself in another passage. Quickly Angsman told Judith his intention of finding Tree, and to stay where she was. He was leaving a candle, and he wouldn't be gone long. She did not look up or reply.

He catfooted to the low connecting shaft and entered the next chamber. It was empty. He crossed quickly to the main tunnel and started up it. Tree, half-animal, would probably feel his way through the darkness with a sure-footed instinct. Angsman moved on carefully, shielding his candle against a chance draft.

Ahead, he heard a pebble rattle. It set up a small clamor of echoes.

He increased his pace, heart pounding. If Tree could reach the rimrock and pull up the ropes, they'd be hopelessly stranded. Also Angsman had left his rifle up there for the descent to the ledge, and Tree could be thinking of that. He might attempt to bargain for his life and the gold.

Daylight rimmed the jagged walls up ahead, and Angsman dropped his candle and scrambled up toward it. He could see the ropes dangling past the cave entrances, saw their telltale little jerks as Tree went up. Angsman lunged the last few yards to grab, too late, at the ropes. A sudden yank whisked them upward.

Stepping onto the ledge he saw Tree on the rim hauling in the lines. The old man gave a burst of crazed laughter. Angsman swung up his pistol, and Tree scrambled swiftly from sight. In a moment he appeared again, pointing the rifle downward. He was breathing hoarsely, his sunken eyes burning behind the tangle of his white hair.

"Greaser stand-off, hoss. You ready to make medicine?"

"No deals —"

"Eh, this child figgered so — want all that yaller gold to yourse'f!"

"Not me, Caleb, you. You killed that boy to keep the secret. I get you back to Stambaugh alive, you'll hang for it."

"Ain't that the truth," Tree jeered softly. "Big if, child. Lessee now. No deal, no gold, an' you'll hunt ol' Caleb down like a dog."

"That's the way of it."

"How you gonna get outa thet hole, child?"

"You forgetting the others? By tomorrow at the latest, Amberley'll be worried enough to come after us. There's other ropes in camp, Caleb."

"Ahuh." Tree's yellow grin was savage. "And you'll be a-hyperin' on my trail." The strain of his growing madness strongly edged his soft words. "Cain't let thet be, hoss."

He stepped backward from view. Angsman stood a puzzled moment, waiting in the sun-blasted stillness. Till he heard the faint grate of rock on rock. Then he knew. Tree meant to start a slide, to seal off the cave. *"Caleb!"*

No answer except Tree's panting grunts as he heaved at a heavy boulder. Angsman saw it tilt out above the rim, and he stepped quickly into the cave mouth.

The massive chunk crashed into the ledge lip, then bounded out and downward. The whole cliffside shuddered and then came a massive ominous rumble. It confirmed his earlier guess. This entire section of wall was faulted, hanging by a hair over a vertical drop where the lower cliff with its old trail had scaled off. Loosened rubble began cascading down.

He cupped his hands to his mouth and shouted, "Caleb! This wall's rotten — you'll bring the whole rim down!"

If Tree heard, he was too far gone to heed. Again his hoarse panting, the grate of heavy rock. A second chunk slammed into the ledge, striking farther inward where it tilted down into the tunnel. The rock angled in with a sudden leap past Angsman, missing him by a couple of feet, then ground to a stop.

The ground trembled. Again the angry rumble.

"Caleb!" His shout was drowned in a thunderous roar. Above it he heard Caleb Tree's thin wail . . . caught in his own trap. Angsman was already retreating deep into the tunnel at a lunging run. He tripped and fell. Then lay hugging the floor as the rimrock avalanched onto the ledge, breaking and spilling over it and into the cave. Pieces of the cave roof fell. The bellow of the ruptured cliff drowned all other sound, but he felt flinty fragments strike his back and legs. As the roar dwindled off, he heard a huge chunk crash not a yard from his head.

Then he was lying quietly in a choking rock-dusted silence. Slowly he opened his eyes, blinking at their sudden sting. He was in utter darkness. He pushed himself up on hands and knees, got to his feet, felt for a wall. He leaned against it, coughing, fighting for breath, till the dust began to settle.

Only then, cold realization flooded him. He and Judith were trapped behind tons of fallen rock.

CHAPTER SIXTEEN

Angsman stood quietly, letting his first panicked knowledge that they were sealed off in a vast catacomb wash away. Methodically he dug out his third and last candle, cupped a flaring match to it. The flame was steady, picking out the clotting slide of rock and debris where the cave mouth had been.

He made his way deeper into the tunnel, paused where he'd hastily dropped his second candle, searching on his knees till he found it. The air should last a good while, long after their last feeble illumination burned out and left them in darkness. Remembering his sensations during those few moments of black silence, it was a thing he didn't want to contemplate.

Now Judith's sobbing cries drifted faintly to his ears, calling his name, and he realized with a shock what her state of mind must be. He called to her, telling her that he was all right, to stay where she was. Groping down the treacherous slant he reached the first chamber and crossed it to the shaft, ducking quickly through. She ran into his arms and he held her tightly, waiting for her hysterical sobbing to ebb away. Then he told her the truth, as gently as he could.

She stepped back slowly and sank to the floor,

staring at her clasped hands in her lap. "We'll die, then. It doesn't matter — nothing matters."

"Watch that talk," he told her sharply. "Start that, you're dead already."

"I am dead already," she whispered. "Don't you see — I've found what I had to be sure of — that I killed Doug."

Angsman carefully pinched out his candle, glanced at the first one's steady flame, then kneeled facing her. Took her by the shoulders, shaking her gently. "Listen to me . . . listen, dammit! Tree killed your brother. Caleb Tree. For the gold. And he's done for. Down at the bottom of that cliff under the rockslide he started —"

He broke off. Her eyes dull and glazed and she was shaking her head back and forth with a pettish little frown that reminded him of a rebuked child in a sleepy tantrum. "You don't understand," she said with soft insistence. "That was only at the beginning. It began a long time ago . . . in Boston. I really killed Doug. This had to be. It's my punishment, don't you see?"

Angsman hesitated only a moment. Then slapped her, and hard. Her mouth fell open and she stared at him in a vaguely shocked way. Her hand lifted halfway to her cheek. He shook her savagely. "Lady, I came a hell of a ways with you and your owl-brother for no pay but wearing and worrying myself near to death. I've killed a man, walked into a hostile 'pache camp, tangled with a feisty buck, got that lunatic Chingo breathing on my neck, holed up in a dead-end ravine, got a cliff pulled down over my head, sweated and swarmed over half the damned country for you, and I'm as much in the dark as when we started on this damnfool junket. Now by God, you're going to tell me what's sticking in your craw!"

His harsh rage, only half-feigned, aroused her at once as he'd intended it should. The pained anger in her face faded to a slow understanding. She gave a weary nod. "All right . . . it can't make any difference."

"It could make a hell of a lot."

He was forcing the shaken girl to a harrowing limit, Angsman knew. But she'd come this far merely to confirm some bleak horror that had haunted her for too long. If she turned from it now, she was lost. She'd go on living with a sick fantasy till it finished her. Under the circumstances, the thought held a wry irony. But in the desert a man came to a hard fatalism concerning life and death. You had no choice as to dying, but there were two ways to finally face it. One way summed up whatever dignity there was in being human.

Judith's words came with halting reluctance, and he began to piece out the truth he'd half-suspected. After her parents were killed, Judith had firmly assumed a responsible role toward her orphaned brothers. Both were quiet-natured and flexible, a fact which had aroused her warm concern. Their backbones had to be stiffened for

201

facing life. Discipline was the answer. But James was already a man, eight years Judith's elder. Though he'd acceded with a mild annoyance to her authority, he was matured enough to be more amused than deeply affected.

With young Doug it was different. Yet, sensitive and shy and indrawn, he'd suffered in silence. For his own good, she'd ordered him about relentlessly, checking every detail of his comings and goings. She'd blinded herself to the changes in them both as the years passed — she becoming a cold and petty tyrant, he turning sullen and more withdrawn.

Then, at nineteen, he'd suddenly rebelled. Against her furious protest, he had gone off to Mexico with Jim. When they returned months later, Judith found that she had lost all control over Douglas. He took to staying out late hours with rough companions or worse; he became cocky and impudent, deliberately mocking her efforts to re-assert authority. One night when he'd come in somewhat the worse for drink, she was waiting for him. He'd taken the tongue-lashing in glaring silence. Then all his pent-up resentment had burst out. He'd cursed her for a meddling old maid; worse, she was cold and sexless, a man in skirts. He'd said other things that had horrified and disgusted her, and then, trembling in cold rage, she had ordered him to leave the house. He'd leave, Douglas promised, and damned if he'd ever come back.

They heard no more of him until six months

later, when Jim received the letter from Santa Fe. It had been a long boastful burst of enthusiasm over his finding of the Obregon map and manuscript, without a single mention of Judith. By now sick with regret and self-loathing, she had realized that the worst thing she could do was interfere further in his life, though Jim told her frankly that Douglas was attempting a thing foolhardy and dangerous.

She had known only too well why Douglas had been driven to this suicidal quest. Despite his bitter repudiation of her, she had succeeded in making him feel like a callow, spineless child. He needed desperately to prove himself to her and Jim and most of all to himself. . . .

As the months went by without word, their worst fears became near-conviction, and with it Judith's aching remorseful feeling of guilt had deepened. For nearly a year she had lived on the edge of apprehension, torn between her desire to learn the truth one way or the other and her fear of widening the break between Douglas and herself if he turned up alive and well. Then Jim's sabbatical leave had come up, and Judith had desperately goaded him into coming west. He'd told her quietly that she was jeopardizing her life for a hopeless needle in a haystack. And yet, understanding, he had offered no objection, and they made the trip.

And now, Judith said in a dull and hopeless voice, she knew the truth. Douglas was dead, and she had killed him.

In the dead silence Angsman rose to his feet. "Stay here," he told her, and crossed past the remains of the conquistadore to the second skeleton, kneeling by it. He pulled out one of the candles and lighted it, holding it low for a careful inspection. There was a round clean hole in the base of the skull where the bullet had gone in. This was what Caleb Tree had known they'd find, the proof that he'd shot Douglas Amberley from behind.

Later, no doubt, Tree had planned to come back with enough mules to pack out the gold. He'd sealed off the main tunnel shaft against chance discovery before he returned. Then, in some way they'd never know, he had sustained the head injury that had turned him into a raving animal. Alone and lacking proper treatment, he had never entirely regained his senses. Even toward the last that was true, Angsman knew, remembering the maniacal frenzy that had cost his life.

Tree had evidently stripped the body of any weapons or useful gear. Frowning, Angsman searched the pockets. He found only a hand-tooled wallet and a leather-bound notebook. Both were dry and cracked, but their contents were preserved perfectly. The wallet contained identification papers and a folded, frayed copy of Obregon's map. Thumbing through the notebook, he realized that it was a journal, with only a few blank pages toward the end. The rest was filled with a tidy, close-written script in pencil, each entry scrupulously dated.

Angsman pocketed both articles, pinched out his candle and stood up, turning his attention to the grim, practical need of dealing with their predicament. There might be another, unknown exit from the caves, for they had penetrated deep into the cliff. But the next step had to be taken carefully; if they went batting blindly about through this maze of tunnels, they'd only lose themselves hopelessly. At least here he had an approximate idea of their position.

He studied the candle on the floor for a slight waver of flame that might betray a draft from one of the converging corridors. There was none, yet there had been a draft before, carried in through the many tunnels. It could only mean that their one possible exit had been choked off. . . .

Steady now, Angsman told himself. He picked up the candle and moved to the nearest tunnel mouth, peering into it. Then to the next. Came to a dead halt, holding his breath. There was no mistaking the sound . . . running water purling its faint echoes up the rocky shaft. He glanced at Judith on her knees staring dully at the floor. He said sharply, "Snap out of it . . . follow me."

The tunnel was cramped and twisting, winding angularly downward at a treacherous pitch. Angsman held their advance to a wary crawl. The sound of rushing water steadily grew. Dropping down and past a sharp bend, they came on it suddenly. An underground stream whose swirling blackness was penciled by the wan glimmers of candle-shed light. The wax cylinder was a mere stub now, singeing Angsman's fingers. He set it down and lighted another, studying the swift current. It cross-angled this narrow tunnel and poured into a second.

It jogged a half-forgotten detail in his mind, and instantly other facts jigsawed into place. Cautious excitement gripped him. He had carefully oriented their advance into the main tunnel from outside, hazarding at the distance covered, noting their left-angling descent at one point. The chamber they had left lay deeply inward, well below and to the left of the former cave entrance. They had continued due west on the continuing downslant of this tunnel. If his rough computing was correct, they were now close to the deep feeder canyon that contained the old Spanish mine, not far from its east wall and almost level to its boxed end. There lay the deep spring-fed pool where their gold-bearing stream had its origin. And maybe the outlet of this subterranean channel.

It was still guesswork, and it would mean taking a dangerous chance. If he were wrong, a drowning death fighting for life would be faster and cleaner than remaining in the caves till they suffocated.

"Can you swim?" he asked suddenly.

"No," Judith murmured dully. Then raised her head sharply, giving him a puzzled look.

He briefly explained, holding the candle low above the water. The flame barely wavered. "Some free air in the water. Not enough to feed these caves. It'll go bad soon enough."

"Could it be any worse?" she whispered.

"You want to live?" he demanded harshly.

A long moment of silence before her almost inaudible sigh. "Strangely, I do. Why do we hold on to life so?"

"You better want it more than that." He paused. "Even if I'm right, it'll be mean going every foot of the way."

"I want it. Will, I want to live."

"All right."

"Can you — swim?"

"Haven't seen that much water since I was a kid, except a muddy river now and again. There was a fine old swimming hole on the farm . . . tell you about it another time."

He flattened on the stony bank and sank his arm into the stream. Its numbing chill took his breath away. Two feet down he touched a pebbly bottom. He lowered himself into the roiling current now, feeling its powerful tug along his legs, then helped Judith to descend. She caught her breath at its icy shock. He led the way down the tunnel, holding her hand tightly, the candle picking out their way.

The water deepened steadily and the rock roof closed down to little more than a foot above their heads. The current was less confined by this deeper channel, its force somewhat weakened. Only this saved them from being swept from their feet as its sullen surge pressed upward from knees to waist. The stream bed underfoot was slick and loose-pebbled, and Angsman felt a knotted tension against the moment when they'd either lose footing in the current or be unable to touch bottom.

The water rose nearly to chest-height as they angled around a stone abutment, and then Angsman halted. The channel ran a straight course ahead for perhaps ten yards, coming to a dead end where the roof tapered gently down to meet the water. He barely made it out by the unsteady flame, and then he twisted back a glance at Judith. Her teeth were chattering uncontrollably, and her face was bloodless. She was standing shoulder-deep in churning water, and he could feel her tight-braced effort to keep footing as she gripped his hand in her own.

"The last lap," he said softly. "We'll know in a minute."

"It's elemental at least." She tried to smile. "Life or death. Don't let go of me, Will. Whatever happens."

"I won't. But it's likely we'll be swimming now. You can't, and I'm no great shucks. I'll keep you up . . . but don't fight me."

He slipped his arm around her waist and they took the last steps, and then his feet flailed into an abrupt dropaway. The candle spat out . . . darkness then. Judith's small scream ended in a splutter. *Don't fight!* He shouted it in her ear, shifting his hold to her shoulders, treading water one-handed and riding the current. It swept them toward the tunnel end they couldn't see. Judith's fingers taloned into his arm with her tense panic, but she did not struggle. In a moment he would be forced to dive . . . how deeply, he didn't know. If the stream did not break through the outside, or if it emerged at too great a distance, or if the last passage was too narrow. . . .

It's elemental at least, Judith had said. With that wry flicker of thought he said quietly, "We're about there. Take a deep breath — hold it."

As he spoke, he strained his eyes downward . . . saw a rippling refraction of daylight break beneath the water.

He dived deeply and strongly toward the pale illusive glitter, knowing it was deeper than it seemed and somewhat wider. The current was tightly confined in its final thrust, and it caught them helplessly as a pair of corks. Angsman felt a bruising blow as his hip struck a jagged rim, and then they were swept through. Shafting sunlight blazed down into the open water. The current turned them head over heels with a final playful nudge, and they were free of it, and he struck upward, his lungs bursting. He broke suddenly to sunlight and air, and they were out; they were free.

CHAPTER SEVENTEEN

They sat on the sun-warmed rock by the pool to rest and catch their breaths. Angsman thought of the wallet and journal; he took the soaked articles from his pocket, pressed them on the rock to remove most of the water, then handed them to Judith. She gave them a listless glance and dropped them at her side.

"I'd look through that journal."

"So that I can read first-hand his feelings for me?" she asked bitterly. "No, thank you."

"You going to face all of it or not?"

She was silent for a full minute, then said wearily, "You're right. But I don't think I can bear to. You read it, please. If there's anything important. . . ."

Angsman picked up the journal and leafed through it slowly, carefully separating the wet pages. He gave a sharp look. "You know he had a girl?"

"Douglas?" She was plainly startled. "He never said a word — but I gave him no reason to confide in me, did I?"

Turning the pages slowly, frowning over each, Angsman pieced out the story of young Amberley's first and only romance. Florence Leighton had been a common waitress in a cafe frequented by Douglas and his wild crowd. A sensitive young girl, it appeared, who had given him the sympathy which he'd found neither in the prison of his home life nor the roistering company of his hard-drinking friends. The early entries were full of Florence, with only a bare mention of his sister — this with a tight and bitter comment that he wouldn't dare bring this working girl to his home.

Angsman flipped on through the pages, coming to the entry relating the final quarrel with Judith. Far from being a bitter note, it contained a burst of wild, boyish exuberance. At last he'd found the courage to make the break and was now free to be his own man. No more of meeting Florence in secret like a skulking coward, no more of loafing off Jim's bounty. He would strike out on his own to the West, land of fresh opportunity; he'd make an archaeological find that would win him wealth and fame and make him worthy of Florence's love.

A man had to pause and smile a little at such romantic idealism. It belonged only to youth, and it touched a mature man with a brief unsettling sadness. The rest of the journal was a straightforward and factual account of Doug's search, his finding of the Obregon *derrotero*, his journey with Caleb Tree into the sierra, finding the Spanish gold diggings — and that was all.

"Doug," Judith whispered, staring blindly at the pool.

"Now you know," Angsman said quietly. "None of it was on your account. All he did was for her."

Judith heaved a deep sigh, shaking her head. Absently she picked up a pebble and tossed it at the pool. "Things aren't that black and white. I played my part, and you know it. I can't escape that, Will."

"Just so you don't try."

She looked at him questioningly, and now he scowled, palmed a pebble and threw it after hers, watching the concentric ripples spread outward. "Once I gave a green second lieutenant some bad advice that helped get a cavalry patrol massacred. Inexcusable carelessness. Point is, I did it with the best intention. I like to think that what I learned has helped keep some good men alive since." He paused thoughtfully. "Once you've made a mistake, you can't take it back. But you can live with it, because it'll hurt you enough to make you live better."

"You — did that? And you seem so sure —"

"Damned carefully sure."

They talked on a while, quietly, and slowly then he saw the wonder of a great budding change in her. It was as though in fronting herself and her guilt, she had found another self she hadn't known existed a warm and knowing person thawing through her lonely armor. And suddenly she said bluntly, "Will — you came of a good home — a gentle upbringing. Why did you leave it for this?"

He shrugged. "Reasons."

"Who was she?"

It startled him, and then he smiled dryly. "No girl. The reason I left was not a very good one, I guess. I hated the stuffy boy's academy Pa packed me off to. Hated being caught in the tight social conventions of the Southern gentry. Thought I was in a trap. I wanted freedom, all I could get of it — ran away from home to find it. Of late I've figured that what I really hated was responsibility — but I gave it a shape of noble rebellion. A kid does that."

"You sound as though it's worn awfully thin."

"Lately, it has."

She sighed, looking into the pool. "Is it wrong for me to suddenly be so happy? Poor Doug. Not even a Christian burial. . . ."

Angsman lifted his glance to the red-walled mesa far above. "Why, I'd say he had the biggest monument in the world. And the one he came to find."

He was silent then, thinking of how they had started this journey poles apart, as a prim Boston lady and a ragtag-and-bobtail frontier loafer, and of how events had moved them toward some middle ground. Somehow he'd become a nostalgic ex-Virginia gentleman, and Judith was learning to be more than a mere lady.

She said nothing for a time, gazing at the pond with a faint, secret smile, and now she drew up her knees and hugged them, and laughed softly.

"I'm still alive, Will. I've done my mourning for Douglas, a year of it, and now it's over. I'm alive and I'm a woman."

Of that fact he'd been strongly and uncomfortably aware for some moments. It was not only that the wet bulky man's trousers and shirt now clung with a loving fidelity to the long slender legs and the two pointed breasts they had indifferently denied, but also that the trim body was drained at last of its icy tensions, softened and relaxed in all its lines.

Unbidden their eyes locked now, and he saw the beginning of a different tension in her, warm-breathing and softly swelling. Her hand moved hesitantly along the rock, and his covered it. They were sitting close, and now they came suddenly together. Some minutes passed, broken only by occasional intervals of breathless murmurs ending impatiently in long heady silences. When they drew apart at last, her eyes were shining with a new, breathless wonder. "Will . . . oh Will." She laughed shakily. "Your beard scratches."

"Beards can be shaved." He added wryly, "I've taken on a lot of rough edges. Some of 'em won't wear off so handily. Can't see myself in a tie and white shirt."

"I'm trying, but neither can I." Her tone was teasing and gently sober. "Suggestions?"

"I got a letter from my brother Joe six months ago. He said that Pa's changed in his mellowing years. Used to be a hard old devil —"

"Are you sure that your running away was all your fault?"

"Well, we scrapped a lot. Mother always took my side, but you didn't argue with Pa."

"I see a certain similarity . . . but go on."

"It seems Joe is busy making quite a name for himself in state politics. Pa and Mother are getting on . . . need somebody to run the farm. Anyway, Pa wants me to come home."

"A gentleman can live with considerably less formality on a farm than in a city, can't he? I've always liked the country."

He said slowly, "It's all pretty sudden."

"I'm not so sure. Will, you didn't do all you've done for us simply because I injured your pride."

"I expect not."

"Is that all?"

"I'm not very eloquent."

"But you are. This way. . . ."

When they arrived back at the cul-de-sac, Ramirez was standing guard at its mouth, impassively ignoring Charbonneau and Ambruster panning the stream. Lately Mexican Tom had walked a straight and sober line, following Angsman's orders to the letter, and the guide felt a kind of wry affection, knowing that Ramirez was fighting all of his irresponsible instincts in holding to his duty while the others gold-grubbed. Because he knew what gold fever could do to a man, Angsman realized how deeply Tom's previous defection had affected him.

Amberley and Pilar came out then, and all of them gathered to listen to Angsman's terse telling of what had happened. Amberley, however, was plainly flabbergasted by the change in his sister. Angsman drew him aside and they talked quietly for a few minutes.

Amberley's thin face broke in a broad, relieved grin. "Now you've enlarged on the situation somewhat, I understand. You and Judith, eh? Wonderful, old man. Congratulations." He thrust out his hand, and Angsman took it, lifting an eyebrow.

"Wasn't sure how you'd take it, professor."

Amberley laughed heartily. "When two people strike sparks from one another, as you did from the first, it's certain that there's more than meets the eye. Now that her mind is cleared of that morbid nonsense, whatever stood between you has been cleared away." He coughed, a shade embarrassedly. "A man's quality shows under stress, Angsman. I've seen yours. Why should I be anything but pleased?"

Angsman said slowly, "Professor, I owe you an apology."

"Oh." Amberley blinked, adjusted his spectacles, and grinned boyishly. "I know. You thought of me as rather a strait-laced fool, an absent-minded bookworm who couldn't see ahead of his nose. In some respects the indictment holds water. Pilar has helped me to understand a good deal that I hadn't, about myself and other people." He coughed again. "We're going to be married, as soon as her family knows."

"Congratulations to you, professor."

"Jim, old man, Jim." Amberley paused soberly. "I'm sorry about Doug, of course, but it only confirms what I'd believed certain. After all we've been through — frankly, for Judith's sake, I'm too relieved to feel sorrow. We've both lived with it too long."

"He took a long chance when he struck out here — reckon he knew that. And figured the risk was worth it, if it was for something he believed." Angsman took out the journal and handed it to the Easterner. "It's all in there, Jim. Your brother died with a purpose."

"It's certain that he hadn't been living with one. It's a good thing to know. Thank you, Will."

Charbonneau sauntered up, chewing a twig in lieu of a cheroot. "Reckon you'll be packin' out now, eh, mes amis?"

"We've got what we came for, Armand. You?"

The Creole's bearded lips twisted wryly around the twig as he took out the poke of gold dust that sagged his pocket, hefting it. "Man don't nevair get enough of this, my fran' Will." He sighed profoundly. "I suppose we got to get, though, before Chingo come. . . ."

They assembled their camp gear hurriedly, loaded their pack animals, heading out from the cul-de-sac and the canyon in a tight group to swing eastward up Obregon Pass. Pilar Torres rode the lineback dun that had been Will-John

Staples's. Angsman moved fifty yards ahead on scout, and Ramirez pulled back an equal distance to the rear; the other three men flanked their mounts to either side of the two women.

Angsman had expected Chingo's move before now, and he knew that their situation was still far from secure. Chingo had now had nearly three days to gather a band of young bloods behind him. And though he would undoubtedly take a long chance to satisfy his thirst for revenge, he was still an Apache. So Angsman, wary of ambush, was scouting out a wide lead on his companions. The Apaches could be following behind, on flank beyond the rim, or holding ahead of their party . . . waiting.

Even if Chingo wasn't yet ready to make his move they were still in the heart of the savage Toscos, with long days ahead. He'd have plenty of time and a hundred ideal points ahead to set up an ambush. Overtaking a party of mounted whites and skirting ahead of them would be no trick at all; in the long pull an Apache buck on foot at his tireless jogtrot could easily distance the strongest horse. Their horses, rested and fresh now, had to be conserved for the grueling trip that still lay ahead.

As they moved on into the late afternoon, the floor of the pass became more rugged with its litter of fallaway rimrock. Because this stretch was ideal for ambush, Angsman slowed pace and made frequent dismounts to check the ground. He paid particular attention to a sandstone buttress hard by the right wall, a perfect lookout point for an Apache scout.

Tramping over to it, a glance told him that someone had laid up here shortly before. The sandstone was pitted and rotten, with a slight abrasion on its surface where a man had leaned his sweaty hand. A faint sifting of loosened sandstone grains covered the spot, still clinging there from moisture.

It meant that Chingo had already laid his deadfall ahead, and that by now his scout had reported their approach. No time to lose . . . the Apaches wouldn't attack after dark, and it was nearly dark now. The impatient Chingo would not wait on tomorrow.

Angsman signaled the others to halt and rode back to them, told what he'd found, and pointed out a natural breastwork of rock he'd already noted under the rim. As Apaches would always try for the horses first to put their enemy afoot, they herded the animals back into a deep protective niche in the wall behind the breastwork. Charbonneau grunted, "W'en you think it come, mon ami?"

"When he knows his ambush failed," Angsman said flatly, "and that'll be shortly, because he'll know how close we were."

The men deployed at yard intervals behind their shallow barricade, Angsman placing the two women toward its rear behind larger rocks after seeing that each was armed with a pistol. As he turned back to join the men, Judith clutched his arm, her eyes wide and strained.

"Suddenly I want to live . . . so much that it frightens me."

"We're not dead yet."

Pilar spoke swiftly, and Judith looked questioningly at Angsman. "She says she'll die before going back to Chingo. Says that you should save a shell too."

Judith moistened her lips. "She should know best. . . ."

They waited in the gathering shadows as the afterglow faded to the first soft touch of dusk, making the light uncertain. This, Angsman knew, would be the ideal moment for Chingo. A minute later he saw the first dark forms slip noiselessly up the pass, flitting from rock to rock. Afterward he caught only brief glimpses, and knew they were coming on at a belly-crawl, slithering almost unseen among the rocks.

Chingo was depending on this first skirmish line of five excellent stalkers to work as close as possible, then rush the barricade and engage the whites at close quarters, Angsman guessed. This would provide momentary diversion necessary for the rest to close the final charge. . . .

"Do you see them? I can't," came Amberley's panicked whisper.

"Yes. Keep your nerve, hold your fire, or you'll be shooting at shadows. Chingo'll want to finish it in one rush, before dark. If that fails —"

He broke off, swinging his rifle quickly toward the right, as a lean form leaped up and sprang

220

for their barricade in long bounds. At the same instant, the other stalkers leaped to sight, charging in a spread-out line. Angsman's rifle roared; the first buck went down in a lunging sprawl. Charbonneau's shot crashed on the heel of his, and Amberley and Ambruster and Ramirez all fired at once. A second man was spun by a shoulder hit, and a third went down with a shattered leg.

The last pair successfully hurdled the barricade, one of them springing on Angsman who tried too late to bring his rifle to bear point-blank; the buck's rush bowled him over.

The other warrior, clearly aware of the white man's protective devotion toward his women, leaped clear past the men and went after the two girls. He reached Judith and caught her by the hair, striking her pistol aside, evidently intending to use her as a shield and pull their attention to him —

Big Turk Ambruster had already dropped his rifle and was lunging after the buck, reaching him an instant after he'd seized Judith. His hands caught the buck's throat, wresting him bodily away from the girl, and they fell together. The warrior fought futilely against the giant's strangling grip. Then a knife flashed in his choppy fist; a moment later the blade was sheathed to the hilt in the big Negro's belly. Ambruster coughed and stiffened . . . put a last crushing effort into his hold.

The first buck, a mere boy, was tussling on

the ground with Angsman; the white scout mercilessly used his greater weight and strength to pin the Apache and disarm him — drew the knife in a quick slash across his throat.

The din of gunfire had filled the pass with crackling echoes. Ramirez and Charbonneau and the Easterner, heeding Angsman's advice as to Chingo's strategy, had held their posts, and now their steady fire had broken the main wave of charging Indians. Amberley had been diverted for only a moment by the second buck's attack on the girls, and then seeing Ambruster take the situation in hand, he crouched shoulder to shoulder with the others, matching their fire.

Angsman gave a swift glance at Ambruster now, saw the giant body slumped silently across his dead opponent. Catching up his ride then, the scout scrambled to the barricade. No more Apaches reached it, though two came close. Charbonneau brought down one at three yards' distance, and the other floundered away on hands and knees, lung-shot.

Already the main body was falling back, carrying wounded fellows, a few rear flankers covering their retreat. In a minute they were gone, fading like ghosts into the lowering dusk.

Three warriors lay sprawled and silent beyond the barricade. Two more lay dead inside it . . . and Turk Ambruster was dead. A reek of burned powder stung the air.

Mexican Tom turned slowly from the breastworks, his rifle slipping from his fingers, a queer, puzzled expression on his long face. *"Por nada,"* he whispered. Angsman caught him as he went down, then saw the clean-welling hole high in the boy's chest.

Ramirez' lips stirred, and Angsman bent his head low to catch the faint whisper: "That meke up a little for my mistake, amigo?" He tried to grin and died in the effort.

CHAPTER EIGHTEEN

Until full dusk closed down, the three men crouched by the barricade, watching and listening. At last their tight vigilance unknotted, and then Amberley rose shakily, his face pale in the dim light, and slipped back to the women. Their voices were dazed murmurs in the silence.

Charbonneau shifted a cramped leg, afterward taking out his poke of gold dust. He poured some of the grains into his palm, muttering under his breath as he held them up near his eyes, studying them with a kind of fevered intensity. Angsman regarded him with a thin weary disgust.

"Armand."

"Ah?"

"Keep a watch."

"Sure, sure," the Creole murmured irritably. He returned the gold to the sack, pocketed it, and picked up his rifle. Angsman left him then, moving back to where Judith knelt by the blanket-covered bodies of Ambruster and Ramirez. Her head was bowed, her lips moving in prayer. She looked up with tears penciling bright streaks on her face.

"Mr. Ambruster died for me, Will."

"It's what he had to do," Angsman said gently.

They had been damned lucky. Rarely was an Apache outfought on his own ground, especially under conditions so favorable. The Apaches had outnumbered the whites, two of them women, by three to one. And they had failed. Only because of Chingo's seething impatience, Angsman's thinking always a step ahead of him, and their successful downing of the two who got past the barricade, had the encounter turned on a hair's balance.

It would badly shake the warriors' confidence for a time, but their next reaction would surely be a vengeful rage. What had promised to be a casual slaughter had turned into a humiliating fiasco, with a serious toll in dead and wounded — a thing these young bucks' seething pride couldn't bear. And the enraged Chingo would be goading them fiercely on to settle the account.

After losing two fighting men like Ramirez and Ambruster, Angsman knew that they could not last another charge. And that charge would come at first light, always the Apaches' favored hour of attack. A few hours' grace while darkness held. They could not kill all of the Apaches, and that left one alternative: kill their whetted thirst for fight and drive them off. It had to be done before they recovered from the first failure.

And there was only one way to do it.

He stood a thin chance of bringing it off. If he failed, Angsman knew, they were as good as dead.

Moonglow shed a silvery cast of almost daylight brightness across cliff and canyon, except for the deep pockets of shadow to which Angsman clung, making his way down-pass. He picked his way in sure-footed silence across the tortured bare rock, where etched contrast of light and dark gave a weird effect of crossing the scarred face of a dead world.

He carried only his knife and Ramirez' old Springfield. Once within shooting distance, he'd need only one long shot. If he missed, there would be time only for a fast retreat, and afterward a hopeless wait till dawn.

The main obstacle was the Apache sentry, and a knife was the quietest and surest way. If he failed to surprise the man and bring him down in silence, or if there were more than one, it would be all up in a minute: that was the calculated risk. In his mind Angsman cursed the moonlight. It would highlight his moving form at every break in the banked shadows. The sentry, standing his watch in immobile alertness, need only fire one shot, and even if it missed, it would alarm Chingo's camp.

He couldn't even be certain that the Apaches had bivouacked in the pass, though that was the logical place. He hadn't yet caught a glimpse of firelight or telltale sound. Ahead lay only a silvered panorama of gilded spires and black swales, craggy and desolate and forbidding even by the softening influence of moonlight.

Angsman moved with every sense straining to alertness.

He came to a dead halt, crouching with rifle braced against his hip. Something detected, or only sensed, pinpointed his attention. Carefully he laid the rifle on the ground, slipped his knife from its sheath and glided toward an abutting boulder by the left wall. As he started up a slight incline to reach it, a dark form detached itself from shadow and sprang like a cat, a knife flashing in its fist.

Angsman pivoted aside, ducking low; the savage knifethrust missed him, and then the hurtling body struck him head on, and they rolled downward in locked battle, thrashing in the moiling silvered dust. Angsman rolled atop his opponent and pinned him. He felt the Apache's blade tear his shirt and glide coldly along his ribs, and then he caught the wiry wrist. The Apache grabbed Angsman's right arm below the elbow.

Moonlight struck the buck's upturned face for one straining instant. The sentry was Matagente. Angsman knew then that the Apache had seen his approach and had deliberately given no alarm, waiting to take his white enemy by knife and finish their quarrel as it had begun, to wipe out the black shame in his mind.

Matagente hissed his fury and heaved wildly upward, rolling them down the last of the incline, he on top now. He fought with all his strength to turn his knife into Angsman's chest. Handicapped by Matagente's leaning weight, Angsman felt his own straining resistance slowly give way. He tried to throw them sideways and only succeeded in bringing the blade nearer his chest. Deadlocked in this spot with his back pinned in a hollow, he knew that his only chance was to get in the first cut.

His knife and arm were cramped against his belly by Matagente's pinioning hand, and now he forced it upward, feeling the buck wince as the keen tip drew a bloody line up his bare stomach and chest to his throat.

With a final furious effort, Matagente thrust all his weight forward and down, driving his blade home. Angsman's desperate wrench on his wrist deflected the knife from above his heart, and then it sank deeply between his ribs. At the same moment Angsman's knife touched Matagente's throat, and then he jerked it in a side-slashing motion. A single gurgling sigh escaped Matagente, the hot wetness of his blood drenching Angsman's arm, and now with a last convulsed shudder his muscles relaxed. Angsman rolled his limp body aside.

Angsman sat up slowly, gripping Matagente's slippery knifeshaft in both hands, wrenching it free. The pain surged high in his right side, and he set his teeth against it, letting its first savage agony ebb away. Afterward he shrugged out of his shirt, tore off his dirty bandanna and made a plug and compress, tying the shirt tightly over it around his chest.

The fight had carried through in a grunting,

panting near-silence. Now he had only to last on his feet till he got above the camp, provided there were no more sentinels. Recovering his rifle, he moved on with dragging steps. It seemed much later that he saw the first tawny wash of flamelight bathe the cliff beyond a gentle bend in the vast cleft.

He made slowly for a crumbled slide of giant rubble off to his right where the bend began. He began to climb it next to the shadowed wall, pausing frequently to rest. He was drenched with sweat and sparks flailed behind his squinted eyelids; every slug of heartbeat against his ribs brought knifelike pain, and the breath soughed in and out of his lungs as though he'd finished a hard run.

Working to the highest point of the slide, Angsman flattened out on its crest, heedless of flinty surfaces gouging his legs and belly. He rested for a panting minute till the distant firelit scene beyond the bend took sure focus in his swimming vision.

It was a small fire that faintly limped the dark lean forms around it, these hunkered down or standing, all fixing a common attention on the squat barrel-chested figure of Chingo. He was speaking volubly and swiftly, matching speech with his dynamic gestures, holding their fascinated stares. Even in this moment, Angsman could feel the drama and tragedy of it: behind Chingo's strange madness lay both brilliant cunning and born leadership. Except for the thing that festered in him, nullifying his native abilities, he might have influenced frontier history for better or worse.

Now he must die, because it was the only way to turn back the others.

An Apache did not run scared, though he'd take sensible flight on those rare occasions when he was surprised by overwhelming odds. His was the ultimate in physical courage. But the supernatural and its grim omens were another matter. A leader was believed to possess strong medicine that would protect him against injury and death. If that medicine went bad, his followers understood that the only course open was instant flight. A strong lieutenant might rally them after a time, but here was only one leader: Chingo.

Laboriously Angsman drew up his rifle and laid the barrel across a rock, painfully shifting his body to settle into his aim. The flickering light was uncertain and Chingo was stalking dramatically back and forth, haranguing his men . . . he took one long step that brought him nearly to the fire. It played over his coppery body naked except for breechclout and high moccasins. He stopped pacing now, pausing with lifted arm in a moment of dramatic emphasis.

Angsman cautioned himself that it was down-slope shooting . . . he allowed for it in taking his sights . . . squeezed off his shot. Chingo was rocked hard on his heels, and in reflex flung back a foot to brace himself, holding erect. Then he toppled forward full length, his still-raised arm falling in the fire. Flying sparks showered his body.

The bucks were utterly frozen for a moment; as the clapping shot echoes died off, one of them rallied enough to bend and turn the leader over. Then he straightened with a wild shout. The dusky forms began scattering off from the firelight, and Angsman waited to see no more.

He pulled down off the slide at a scrambling run, falling twice. At its bottom he headed back at a stumbling weary trot. The others, tensely waiting, would know the meaning of that single shot, followed by no others: either he or Chingo was dead. Though he'd ordered them to remain where they were, very likely they would come to meet him. Angsman hoped so, because he doubted that he had enough to make it back. . . .

CHAPTER NINETEEN

While darkness held, they waited in hopeful un-
certainty, and when no Apache attack came at
dawn they knew that Angsman's one-man sortie
had paid off. To make sure, Armand Charbonneau trekked down pass to where the Apache
bivouac had been. Shortly he returned to confirm it: the Apaches had apparently pulled back
for good. The body of Chingo was gone, and
Charbonneau had displayed himself boldly to
any concealed sniper. No bullet or arrow had
answered his rashness. . . .

It was Amberley who, after the rifle shot had
come, had left shelter and moved cautiously
down the pass. For all they knew a sentry might
have shot Angsman; he might be badly hurt and
unable to get back. Two hundred yards up the
pass he'd found the scout's sprawled form, and
afterward toted him back to the barricade across
his shoulders. There Amberley had expertly
cleaned and treated the wound. The sting of
carbolic revived him, and against Judith's objection he sat upright while Amberley affixed a
bandage.

Matagente's last ferocious try had not inflicted so deep a cut as Angsman himself had
supposed; its force was deflected by the glancing

slash along his ribs before it entered between two of them. No vital organ had been touched. His strength had been sapped from loss of blood pumped away in his effort to reach the slide, then by his stumbling retreat. He got some restless sleep, and by morning was running a slight fever; he felt clearheaded enough.

Against Judith's concern now, Angsman insisted that they move on at once. The Apaches would shun them for a while, it being plain that their medicine was stronger, but while they remained here their presence would be an angry goad to the young bucks. A few wild ones might take the bit in their teeth. Also they'd want to recover the bodies of their dead from this place.

Within the hour they were packed and saddled, moving on with Judith flanking Angsman; Pilar Torres and Amberley brought up the rear. Charbonneau took the lead, riding well ahead.

Through the shimmering dead heat of the long day, they were held to a slow pace. Angsman's brains seemed to boil moltenly in his head. He was drenched with sweat, and every hooffall of his animal over uneven ground brought stabbing pain. As the day wore on, he felt a hot trickle under his shirt and knew that his wound had opened again. It patched a slow stain against his shirt, and he was glad it was on the side away from Judith. He held straight in the saddle, giving the rest no hint of his condition, and feverishly wondered if this day would ever end.

In spite of which he kept a watchful eye on Charbonneau. The Creole rode leisurely ahead, occasionally with a lanky leg cocked around his saddle horn. From time to time he took out his gold pouch and spilled some of its contents into his hand. Once he took out another that had been jammed out of sight inside his shirt. No doubt Ambruster's, relieved of his dead body when they'd buried the Negro and Ramirez this morning before setting out. . . .

It was a natural thing to do, but knowing Charbonneau, Angsman's unrelaxed suspicion was heightened. There was something feverish and obsessive to the way the Creole kept poring over the gold dust. That lust had destroyed plenty of good men; Charbonneau already had the moral fiber of a rattlesnake. For hours, too, the ebullient Creole had held a strangely brooding silence. Angsman steadily watched the back of his lean head with its greasy queued hair beneath a battered slouch hat, wondering exactly what was passing through it.

At dusk they made an early halt at a good camp site in the flanking boulders. Here, Amberley said firmly, they could rest for a day or so until Angsman recovered some strength. He helped the scout to the ground, and eased him over to a low rock where he seated himself. By now he was so intent on Charbonneau that he wholly ignored Judith's shocked scolding when she saw his bloody shirt, and she broke off in a hurt silence. Charbonneau casually heaved the packs off their animals. Then as, without a word, he started rummaging through Angsman's own things, the scout reached awkwardly, wincing, for the gun holstered at his right hip.

Instantly Charbonneau wheeled erect, his gun in fist. "I wouldn', mon ami . . . you 'ave no chance. Pull the gun slowly an' throw it away — you too, professair — that is it."

As Amberley mechanically obeyed, he could only stare for an uncomprehending moment, then got out, "What's the meaning of this?"

"Ask your so-fine guide. Armand is through with the talk, through with the waiting."

"What do you mean?" Judith whispered. "What do you want?"

Charbonneau had Angsman's pack open, and now he stooped without taking his eyes off them, came up with a heavy leather sack in his fist. "This for now, Ma'mselle. . . ." He shoved it in his coat pocket.

"But that's Ramirez' gold Will is saving for his widow —"

"Of this I would not worry, Ma'mselle . . . eh, Will?"

Angsman, watching him steadily, said nothing, and then Judith cried, "Will, what does he mean?"

"He wants all the gold," Angsman said softly. "The lode back in those cliffs — the *cargas* the Spaniards left in the caves — all of it."

Charbonneau's shoulders heaved with a fevered chuckle. "W'at I tal' you, Ma'mselle? That

Will, he don' miss nothin'."

"Besides him, the four of us are the only ones who know . . . and we've got the only copies of the old map."

"My God," Amberley said tonelessly, "he wouldn't — not women —"

"A transplanted Southerner, once a gentleman," Angsman murmured. "A frontier man now . . . seems like everything would go against it. In his right mind, it would. And he'd take our word not to tell anyone about the gold. But he's lost his right mind, Jim. Look at him."

Charbonneau's faint grin faded; his eyes burned like coals as he tilted his gun an inch to bear on Angsman. "You *Americain* cochon —"

"Charbonneau, listen," Amberley pleaded, spreading his hands. "Listen, man. The Spanish gold is buried in those caves for good. You can't get the rest with the Apaches back there. Bonito won't tolerate any more gold-seekers; he told Will as much. Without those considerations, how do you expect to mine and transport it out — alone?"

"Ahh . . . always he is the logical scholair, my fran' James. Ah. But Armand 'ave a little upstairs, too. The Bonito, he is ver' old *sauvage,* n'est-ce pas? He will live only a little while. Then his people, they will not 'old out longair; they will come in to resairvation like good Apach'. Armand will then return, with the mules, the dynamite and the quicksilvair, the tools; he will blast and sluice and dig; alone he will take out the fortune of Croesus — and share with no one. Ha!"

A muscle twitched in Charbonneau's jaw as he talked; sweat glistened on his face and the gun he held trembled. Angsman thought, Gone completely out of his head with it. It'll kill him sure before he's done . . . but too late to do us any good.

Now the final decision was taking wicked shape on the Creole's gaunt face, his gun lifting to center squarely on Angsman's chest. For a wild moment Angsman felt his thoughts thread out against a blank wall, and then he thought coldly: Delay him . . . buffalo him.

He glanced quickly at Pilar, spoke in swift Spanish, to the effect that it was a fine day without rain in prospect.

Charbonneau, knowing only the crudest Mexican argot, scowled and half-lowered the gun. "Eh? W'at you say?" Swiftly he wheeled, covering the Spanish girl. "Wa't you tell her?"

"She doesn't savvy Yankee. I was telling her you mean to kill us. To say any prayers she knows."

"You lie!" Charbonneau strode forward, black fury boiling in his face. He stopped in his tracks with a dreamy and relaxed smile. "Ah-ha. You try to throw Armand off the guard, so one of you make the try for me." He laughed harshly, suddenly raised a foot and set it against Angsman's chest with a brutal thrust that drove him sideways off the rock. He fell on his back with a grunt of pain.

Charbonneau roared. "Ho, look at you, the great white scout; weak as a 'ousecat. Look at all of you!" He spun on a heel, swinging his gun in a wild arc toward the others. "A Yankee scholair too absent of the mind to find his way outside a book . . . his silly love-struck sistair . . . a goddam greaser girl likely *enceinte* with an 'alf-Apach' brat for all her lies." He spat sideways. "I should not 'ave to waste the bullet on such dumb useless cochon; they nevair find their way out of the mountain without you —"

As the Creole's attention had partly veered from him, Angsman doubled his knees and inched his prone body forward a few cautious inches, fighting the pain of it. Even as Charbonneau swung back to him, he straightened his legs in a savage kick. His feet struck the Creole above the ankles, knocking his feet from under him. He fell to his knees with an explosive curse. *"Sacre —"*

As Amberley lunged at him, Charbonneau surged to his feet, hissing his inarticulate fury. He swung his gun in a short savage arc. In mid-lunge, Amberley tried to halt and fling up his arms, but the muzzle caught him across the temple. He fell without a sound.

With straining haste Angsman had already rolled on his belly, then came up on his knees, floundering to reach and grab Charbonneau's belt. He strengthened his hard tug with a back-

238

ward heave of his body. Yanked off-balance Charbonneau fell solidly atop him, and in the crushing pain of it, Angsman's senses momentarily blacked away. Charbonneau's curses were a distant roar in his ears, and then he could see again, felt the Creole's weight straddling him. Charbonneau's lips peeled off his teeth as he held the pistol an inch from the scout's face, cocked it. Angsman caught his wrist in both hands and twisted the gun sideways.

Slowly Charbonneau forced it back against his weak hold, and Angsman put out a last weary effort, watching the barrel slide into line with his right eye. Beyond it lay Charbonneau's blood-swollen face, and over his shoulder then Angsman saw Judith stoop quickly, come up with a pistol in her hand. She pointed it at Charbonneau's back, and Angsman tried to shout, *Hammer it back!* but the words were a strangled gasp. Then he saw the pale horror in her face and understood her hesitation.

Pilar did not hesitate. She snatched the gun from Judith, held it at arm's length in both hands, double-thumbing the hammer. The shot was like a flat hard blow . . . its echoes trailed into a stunning silence.

Angsman used his last strength to roll away Charbonneau's limp body, turning it face down. The bullet had emerged from his face, but the hole where it went in was small and clean.

Judith sank to her knees, burying her face in her hands, and Angsman lay on his side, panting, resting a moment so that he could move to her and tell her it was all right. Amberley groaned and tried to sit up, and Pilar pressed him back, saying calmly, soothingly, "Rest a little, Jaime; do not try to move . . . everything is fine."

Long days afterward, four people halted to rest their horses on a last long rise of land. The squat adobe shape of Fort Stambaugh still lay distant on the flats, but it seemed very near now. Behind it the Pinos River crawled like a sinuous brown snake down to the shabby sprawl of Contention-ville. Here at last lay the first links with the civilization to which they were coming home.

Home. The word had a strange sound in Will Angsman's mind, but it was a good one.

He helped Judith to dismount, watching her face. It was sun-darkened and thinned and dust-filmed, and she was very tired, he knew, with a deeper exhaustion than she'd ever known. Still, she summoned a smile for him, and he decided that she was quite beautiful. He thought this, knowing another man would think him a fool, and not caring.

He uncapped his canteen and handed it to her, and she drank deeply. Lowering it then, she surprised him looking off toward the hot, lonely wastes they had crossed. Aware of her sober gaze, he grinned, took the canteen and drank.

"You were thinking that this was the last time for you . . . out there," Judith said quietly.

"That's done with."

"But it gave you something good, that life. Something I'll never know. Perhaps a disciplined toughness — to face anything." She bit her lip, glancing at her brother and Pilar who stood off a little distance by their horses, their voices quiet murmurs. "I always prided myself on being strong. Then, after facing what I had to, about Doug, I'd thought that I could bear up under anything. Yet a little Spanish girl of nineteen showed me for a weak, preening —"

Angsman put an arm around her, shook her gently. "Anyone can take buck fever. You saw Pilar cry later on . . . she's not so hard as all that. All she's been through would toughen someone for anything, if they lived through it."

"But I failed you, Will, when you needed me most —"

"Failed to kill a man? You don't want to think like that. Right or not, a thing like that marks you where it doesn't show. She'll have to live it for a long time. I know."

She nodded and was silent. He sensed the lingering trouble behind her still face, and wondered if she were still brooding on it. But she said softly, "I saw the look in your face a minute ago. Will, are you sure that you'll never want to go back? Perhaps for the gold?"

"That's blood gold, Judith. Killed everyone who touched it, from Obregon through Charbonneau. I've already burned both maps — Doug's and Jim's. We've got Ramirez' gold, Charbonneau's and Ambruster's . . . it'll all go

241

to Tom's wife, Lupe. Let the rest stay where it is — it'll be found again." He shook his head bleakly. "In some ways the Apaches show a damn' sight more sense than us."

He saw the wistful question still touching her expression, as though she thought that a part of him she'd never know would remain here. He considered that, looking back toward the hazy line of far sierra. No . . . why should it? A man was himself the holder of the parts, of all he'd been and seen and done; if he didn't regret any of it, he would lose nothing, for the best of it would stay with him.

"No regrets," he told her gently. "Let's get on. We'll make the fort before nightfall."

Mounting again, they put their horses down the long slope.